THE PISSERS' THEATRE

THE PISSERS' THEATRE

eckhard gerdes

Black Scat Books

2021

THE PISSERS' THEATRE

Eckhard Gerdes

ISBN-13 978-1-7357646-9-6

BLACK SCAT BOOKS
Publishers of Sublime Art & Literature
BlackScatBooks.com

I would like to acknowledge the support and assistance of my daughter Penelope and my friends Amy Kurman and Derek Pell in reading and responding to the book in manuscript. Without their suggestions, this would have been a lesser book.

"EVERYBODY'S LIFE IS BEING FILMED in 3D so that it can be played back for eternity." Thus spoke Karen Zurück to her friend Kay Cera as they entered the theatre. "That's why I prefer going to plays. Everyone's attention is on the actors, so no one is actually filming me."

"How do you know?" asked Kay. "They could have CCTV filming everyone."

"A friend of mine does the lighting for this theatre, and he told me that they did not have CCTV."

"Ah, that's good to know. I hope the play is not too disgusting. The title worries me."

"*The Pissers' Theatre*? I don't really know anything about it. Tonight is the premiere, so no reviews have even been published."

A young usher, a man in his early twenties, approached Karen. "Ma'am," he said, "we'll need you to remove your hat inside the theatre." Karen was wearing an enormous saucer disc hatinator in the design of a slice of watermelon, the red of which was set off beautifully by her long green evening gown.

"Why?" she asked.

"People sitting behind you will not be able to see over you," replied the usher.

"What is your name, young man?" asked Karen.

"Rayro," replied the young man.

"Rayro, you have to understand that putting on and removing

this, which by the way is not a hat but is actually a *hatinator*, is quite difficult. Couldn't you just seat us somewhere where no one is sitting behind us? Perhaps in the back row?"

Rayro scrunched up his face in a display of frustration and said, "I am sorry, Ma'am, but the back row sold out first. It seems to be our most popular row for this show."

"Goodness," interjected Kay, who was slightly older than Karen and who sometimes felt that she had the obligation of a big sister to help Karen in awkward social situations. "That makes no sense. This isn't a Gallagher show, is it? I mean, no comedian is coming out and smashing fruit that will spray over everyone in the front rows, is he?"

"No, Ma'am. But this is, as the name of the play suggests, a pissers' play."

"Oh, good God," exclaimed Karen. "The actors are going to pee on the audience? Who was he, GG Allin, who used to do that? Yuck. Kay, we should probably leave if that's the case. I don't want anyone to pee on me. I'm not the President."

Kay laughed.

"No, Ma'am. I assure you that will not happen. The show is for elderly patrons who have difficulties sitting through performances without having to get up to use the facilities."

"Isn't that every play nowadays?" said Kay, sarcastically.

"Not really. We have set up the seats so that patrons can press a button when they need to go. A buzzer sounds, and the actors stop right away, mid-scene even, so that the patron can get up and leave and then return without having missed anything. When the patron returns, the actors pick up from where they left off."

Karen seemed shocked. "That suggests that the play might take a while. What if forty patrons have to leave?"

"Then the actors will pause forty times."

"Why don't they all just wear Depends?" asked Kay.

"That's not the way the show works," answered Rayro. "The Playbill explains all that." He handed each woman a Playbill. "I can seat you in one of the loge boxes. Because of their distance from the washrooms, those have gone unsold."

"That would be perfect for us," said Kay. "Thank you."

Rayro, just to be extra helpful, led the women to their seats on the loge level and then returned to his post by the theatre entrance.

"He seemed like a nice young man," said Kay.

"I suppose." Karen opened her Playbill and turned to the list of *dramatis personae* and the actors who were to play them.

One, a wealthy socialite known as Mary Widow, was known by the nickname "Typhoon Mary." She was listed first, so Karen figured she must be the primary character in the play. In her company was a man named Henry Scriptorem, known as "Henry the Hack." He was described as a friend of Mary, the man who not only acted in but also wrote the play-inside-the-play, also called *The Pissers' Theatre*. Karen was wondering if this was yet another postmodern metaplay about a play.

Kay was reading her Playbill, too. "It looks like the play only has the two main characters, who are playing people who are acting in a play that an audience on the stage is watching."

"Oh, gosh. I think you are right. I didn't know this would be something *post*modern. I guess the many breaks in the play might be welcome after all," replied Karen. "Maybe the four audience members in the play will bring some life to it."

"One can hope."

The house lights went off and then back on again, signaling that the play was about to begin. Karen and Kay settled into their seats and hoped for the best.

* * *

CHARACTERS
MARY, 50ish
HENRY, 60ish
FOUR RANDOM AUDIENCE MEMBERS

TIME
The present, late afternoon

PLACE
Mary's third-floor apartment in Rogers Park, Chicago.

A large dining room table sits squarely in the middle of the room. On the table are stacks of papers, pens, a shoe box, and a large-scale dollhouse-sized replica of a theatre with seats and a stage. A door to the apartment is off to the side, with a coat rack standing next to it.

Scene I-1: Mary has an idea

MARY is sitting at the table. She is staring at a yellow pad of notepaper as HENRY enters, quietly, hanging up his coat on the rack next to Mary's.

HENRY
How's it going, Mary? You look befuddled. Are you flummoxed?

MARY
No, I'm not. I've been staring at this sheet of paper for an hour, but I can't come up with anything.

HENRY
That's because I wasn't here to help. No ideas yet?

MARY
Not really. But this has to be a play for older patrons. I am stumped. I don't want to talk down to the

elderly, but we have to take their physical limitations into account.

HENRY

Like what?

> (HENRY sits down behind the theatre model, reaches into the shoebox, and pulls out a miniature figurine of a seated patron. He places it onto one of the miniature seats.)

HENRY (cont'd)

Do you mean like their hearing issues?

MARY

That and other bodily challenges they may have.

HENRY

What? Like urination?

> (MARY points to the model.)

MARY

> (winces noticeably.)

Imagine this is the theatre. From here, the nearest washrooms are all the way over here.

> (MARY gets up and walks to the far end of the table and puts her finger down onto a spot on the tabletop.)

HENRY

That's a problem, for sure. But don't most of them wear diapers?

MARY

I don't know, but I don't want them to have to sit in their own urine. That's horrible, and it will make the theatre smell funny.

HENRY

I'm not so sure. I think the technology for adult diapers has really improved over the years. I'm even looking forward to wearing them myself someday.

(MARY doesn't take the bait.)

HENRY (cont'd)

I'm just kidding. I don't think that. But we have to be able to make the experience a positive one for them.

MARY

Henry, stop it! We need to get this done!

HENRY

Well, let's do something to accommodate their needs.

MARY

Okay. I'll go talk to Mr. Robbins again. He can tell us what we can and cannot do to his theatre for the play.

(MARY picks up the seated patron and moves him to another seat)

HENRY

I'm sure we'll get it all taken care of. He knows we need to design the set to match the play.

MARY

Of course, but I think we need to make modifications to the seating, not just to the stage set.

HENRY

What do you have in mind?

MARY

I'm not exactly sure yet, Henry. I want the patrons to be able to pee freely, I guess, without having to miss any of the play.

HENRY

Well, that'll be a challenge.

MARY

Yep.

(MARY gets up and pulls her coat off the coatrack by the door.)

I made some mac and cheese earlier. The leftovers are in the fridge, if you'd like some. I should be back in a couple of hours.

HENRY

Relax, Mary. I'm sure we'll figure out something.

(MARY shrugs and then exits and closes the door behind herself)

* * *

That was when the buzzer went off for the first time. Fortunately the actors had finished the scene. Henry calmly left the stage, which was left lit and unoccupied until the next scene could begin.

Kay looked over at Karen to see what Karen's reaction was. Karen looked somewhat annoyed.

"You okay, Karen?"

"That wasn't much so far. We'd only barely begun."

"Yeah, this is going to be a long play at this rate."

"Or maybe it's a short play that is going to take a long time."

"Yeah, that's probably it. I hope so. If it's a long play, this will make it seem like an eternity, like that *Titanic* movie, which seemed fifteen hours long."

"It did."

"Good thing that Aristotle's *Poetics* weren't being applied in that."

"What do you mean, Kay?"

"I mean, in Greek tragedies, the climax came in the middle of the play. Can you image, after the climax, half of *Titanic* would still be coming? That'd be four hours of them floating in the ocean. Jack might ask, after a half hour of treading water, if he might have a turn to float on the driftwood. Rose would say, 'No. You're the man. You must drown.'"

"Hah! We don't know that. After another half hour, she might have felt guilty that she was resting while Jack was treading water, and she might have offered to switch for a while. Or maybe they could both have hung on to the driftwood and gone in search of another piece so that both could float."

"Ha ha. I'll be back in a minute. I am going to see if I can beat the crowd to the washroom. Power of suggestion…."

"Okay. See you," said Karen, returning her attention to her Playbill. She looked at the map of the facility that was inside the back cover.

"Kay, actually on this map they show that we do have a washroom on this loge level after all. I wonder why Rayro didn't mention it?"

"It's probably exclusive for the loge bougies. I'll inspect it."

Once there, Kay found herself in a short line for the ladies' room. As she waited, she fell into conversation with the woman ahead of her, a smallish woman wearing a blue seersucker dress. At the theatre! Kay figured she couldn't be a regular theatre-goer.

"What do you think of the play so far?" asked Kay.

"It's hard to tell. It barely got started."

Kay looked at the clock on the hallway wall. "I hope whoever is in there won't be too long," she said.

"She will be. That's my mother. I'm sorry."

"No problem. I just timed my having to go rather poorly."

"I think my mom timed her visit to the washroom pretty well. I'm Kate Levertov, by the way," she said. "Nice to meet you. You come to a lot of plays?"

"Hi, Kate. I'm Kay Cera. Yeah, my friend and I come a couple of times a year. We have friends who have season passes but who are too busy to use them as often as they'd like."

"Kay Cera? Any relation to Michael?"

"Oh, no. None at all, but I do like his work, especially *Scott Pilgrim*."

"That was very good. I also liked him in *Superbad*."

"Yes, that was also very good." Just then Kate's mother emerged from the washroom. Kay wondered how a theatre could make do with such a small washroom, but then she remembered that this was the "exclusive" washroom. She went in and immediately regretted having done so. The old lady had left somewhat of a mess and had not cleaned up after herself, so Kay had to do it in order to use the seat. Fortunately she always carried disinfectant wipes in her purse for just such an eventuality.

Meanwhile, Karen read the actors' biographies. Aloysius Truman, who played Henry Scriptorem, was the grandson of a Holocaust survivor who had been forced to perform music for the concentration camp Nazis. He had been a cellist, and family legend said that he'd played with violinist Viktor Frankl in the Auschwitz string quartet. Aloysius's passion for music came from his grandfather, and musical performance led Aloysius to his passion for theatrical performance. He had been active in his community theatre, and that led to his involvement in the resident theatre repertory company at the Screaming Yellow Zonkers Theatre on Broadway in Chicago. Mindy Ginter, besides being the star of the performance, was a noted Chicago socialite and philanthropist. She was also the executive producer of *The Pissers' Theatre*. Her theatrical credits involved local performances in plays by Ibsen, Ionesco, Beckett, and Pinter, all of which she played the female lead in, and all of which she was the executive producer of. She had been nominated for a Joseph Jefferson Award for her performance in the Chicago cast of *The Unsinkable Molly Brown*. One local reviewer said that "Chicago owes a great debt to Ms. Ginter for her passionate portrayal," but he was probably even more grateful for her support of that reviewer's theatre column, which somehow always seemed to attract a great amount of advertising revenue from businesses that Ginter was involved with. Karen had noticed those ads in the newspaper more than two years earlier, and the fact that Ginter was the spokesmodel for several of those companies had certainly taken her attention.

Just then Kay returned, and the lights flicked off and back on to let people know the play would be resuming.

* * *

Scene I-2: Henry has an idea, too.

(HENRY is sitting at the table. He is staring at the yellow pad of notepaper)

HENRY
(talking to himself)

How's it going, Mary? You look befuddled. Are you flummoxed? Why do I always say such stupid things? What I really should have told her is that I enjoy working alongside her.

(HENRY picks up the patron figurine and looks
at it closely.)

How are we going to be able to set up the theatre for
the incontinent? There must be an easier way.

(HENRY reaches into the shoe box and pulls
out a handful of other seated patron figurines,
which he begins to place onto the miniature
theatre seats. As he does so, four actors carrying
folding chairs enter the stage and place their
chairs facing HENRY, with their backs to the
audience. They seat themselves.)

HENRY (cont'd)

This won't work. They won't have any privacy. Everyone will know who pushed the button.

(MARY enters. HENRY claps, which makes
the four audience members clap. MARY seems
taken aback.)

HENRY (cont'd)

Mary! I think I may have an idea!

MARY

I think I have one, too.

(MARY and HENRY hunch over the dollhouse
together. They pull figurines out of the shoebox
and place them on the dollhouse theatre stage
and in the miniature audience.)

* * *

The buzzer went off again. Mindy and Aloysius calmly stood
up and walked off stage. Aloysius reached into his shirt pocket
for a cigarette. Mindy noticed and grimaced. She hated when

Aloysius smelled of cigarette smoke. She had to try to ignore it, or she'd gag.

Kay turned to Karen and shrugged. "Well, this is going to take a while, isn't it?" she asked rhetorically.

Karen reached two fingers into her handbag and extracted her phone. She opened a game.

Kay's eyes lit up. "What are you doing?'

"Gardening. If I don't water my flowers every six hours, they die."

Kay shook her head and looked away.

Player arrives at the goats of a mythic flower. A patch in the crate spins, and the ice of an old pissoir can be seen.

HERO: I need to learn to locate the bathroom.

BATHROOM ATTENDANT: Please tell me how you intend to pay for such lessons.

If the player has the COWBELL OF PROCURANCE, proceed to scene #42, otherwise turn away!

"Karen, stop! You can play games later. We have a problem to solve before the play begins again."

Karen put away her phone. "Okay, I'm listening."

"I think that they are responding to pee-er pressure." Kay looked askance sheepishly at Karen, which Karen took to be a sign of sarcasm.

"Ha ha!" Karen didn't know what else to say.

"You know, my job is not to evaluate *what* you have to say as much as it is to evaluate *how* you say it," said Kay.

Karen scrunched up her face in a show of confusion.

"So you can tell me if *how* I say anything confuses you," prodded Kay.

"No, I'm not confused. No worries."

"Okay, just checking. Oh, look. They are finally starting again. This is *so* time-consuming. There must be a better way."

"Shhh! It's starting."

The lights went down, and music played. "You're into Something Good" by Peter Kin-Eater began and then faded out after the first chorus....

"Urine to something good?" joked Kay.

"Shhh!" admonished Karen yet again.

* * *

Scene I-3: Mary has concerns

(HENRY and MARY are sitting at the table. They are comparing notes written on the yellow pad of notepaper that had been in front of MARY.)

HENRY

I think we can reconfigure the theatre this way.

(HENRY points to a drawing on the pad.)

If we slant the floor more steeply so that the people in the back can see okay, then I think this will work. Every filmgoer should be able to see over the stall in front of them.

MARY

(shakes her head.)

Oh, gosh. This looks very expensive. We will have to not only incur a massive bill for reconfiguring the floor and installing all the individual toilet booths, but the cost of the plumbing will be insane.

HENRY

True, but think of how well this will work over the long term. We will be the favorite theatre of the elderly throughout the city.

MARY

We can't afford this. Even if it does make a return on the investment in a couple of years. That is a lot of cash to float on the flimsy raft of possibility.

HENRY

You can afford it, Mary. You are not exactly poor, you know.

MARY

And I plan to stay that way. This looks like it might really hurt me if it goes south.

HENRY

It won't. We have been over this carefully. I am sure you have enough in your Scrooge McDuck counting house to pay for it.
(He chuckles)
And in a few years, this will all have paid for itself through increased revenues.

MARY

I think you think I am a lot richer than I am. We need to see how we can cut costs.

HENRY

Of course. I have one idea already. If the patrons get to sit on their own private thrones, we should make sure that they only use them for liquid waste. We will have regular toilets for solid waste out in the halls, as normal. But we want to avoid a stench in the theatre, and we also want to avoid loud, repeated flushing noises. I think we can—

* * *

This time the buzzer interrupted the scene. Mindy and Aloysius just stayed at the table and waited for the patron to return. Aloysius called to a stagehand and asked for a paper. The stagehand brought out an enormous Sunday edition newspaper and handed it to Aloysius. Mindy asked Aloysius for the lifestyles section, so he pulled that out and handed it to her. The crossword puzzle was in the lifestyles section. Mindy opened up to the crossword and began working on it while they waited. Aloysius began reading the front page.

"A sixteen-letter word for when a person has a low level of attentiveness?"

"Easy. Absentmindedness."

"What?"

"Hardy har har…. Exactly."

* * *

The play had been going on for a while before Kay and Karen realized it was back on. They were sitting in their seats, lost in their own thoughts.

Karen was remembering her dream from the night before. She'd been in a large urban university that was several floors high. She'd taken her family to the fourth floor, to her department, and asked them to stay while she went to the fifth floor, which had the closest women's room. When she returned, they were all gone. She knew instinctively that the rest of her family had ditched her. That didn't feel good.

She spent the rest of the time looking for them, but she quickly realized that she knew very little about the institution for which she worked. The secret rooms led to secrets that people did not want exposed.

That didn't really interest her. She tended to look at details in a binary way. Would this hurt me, or would it help me? The tougher question was "for what"?

Kay returned from the washroom again. "That washroom is disgusting," she said. "I should call the Board of Health on this one."

"I am sure they have been scrutinizing everywhere since the pandemic."

"Yeah, I guess. So what have you been doing during this period?"

"Oh, I've been reading experimental fiction, of course. Haven't you?"

"Uh, what's that?"

Karen rolled her eyes. They hit the bank and turned up snake eyes. "I" is not a pronoun one can ignore forever. For "ever" is an age that one would only want to reach if one could have one's youth and health along with it.

"Are you okay, Karen? Your pupils look huge."

"Yeah, my eyes are wide open." Then she began to sing, *I can see for miles*....

"Shhh! Karen, we're at the theatre."

"Oh, sorry. This stopping and starting again is a hard groove to get into."

Then she thought about what Kay had said. Why shouldn't we be singing at the theatre? Isn't that exactly the best place to sing? But then she felt ill and had to rush to the washroom. To be spiteful, as she got up, she pushed the pause button so the play would be delayed again.

In the toilet, flushing her vomit, she thought that a solution to the problems of the world could be found, and she knew she was on the right track.

However, when morning came, she would have forgotten all

about it. But she would feel cleansed somehow, as if everything that had happened the night before was a moment of catharsis.

She began to worry about what Kay would think, so she flushed again, left the stall, and with as much dignity as possible, washed her face in the sink. She had a small travel bottle of mouthwash that she always kept in her purse, so she rinsed the taste of vomit out of her mouth with that and prepared to face whoever was on the other side of the bathroom door.

* * *

When the house lights and the loud canned music came on, Mindy and Aloysius just stayed at the table and shot the breeze. Aloysius mentioned he liked comic books and had a hankering to write a few. Mindy snickered, but Aloysius told her he was serious. He had a superhero character he'd thought of. She asked what the hero's name was, and when Aloysius said, "The Brown Streak," Mindy looked like she'd been suddenly told she was going to die.

"You didn't just say that."

"Why?"

"You're an idiot."

"What?"

"Not only is that disgusting, but that hero already exists in *Grand Theft Auto*."

"Oh. I didn't know."

"You didn't know it was disgusting?"

"No, I didn't know someone else had beaten me to it."

"If it's scatological humor, someone else has already thought of it. I guarantee that."

* * *

On the other side of the door stood Rayro, looking over the

railing down to the main floor of the lobby. He turned when he sensed Karen's movement behind him. When he recognized who she was, he turned his attention back to the main floor.

Karen walked up to him and asked him, "See anything interesting?"

Rayro smiled. "Yes, Ma'am. It's all interesting."

"Please call me Karen."

"I can do that. Is that your name?"

What? Why would I say that otherwise?

"Yes. I am Karen, *Rayro*. Is your name really 'Rayro'?"

"No, it's really Raymond Robert, but Ray was my father. He was Raymond Francis, so rather than calling me Ray or Ray Jr., my folks decided to call me Rayro, and it stuck." He was a bit annoyed at having to repeat this explanation for the five-hundredth time. "Ma'am?"

"Karen," she said sharply.

"Karen, I think you need to return to your seat. The sign is up for the play to resume."

"Thanks, Raymond."

"Rayro."

"If that's what people say."

He looked a bit confused by that retort, so his attention turned to anything other than her.

Karen found her seat, and Kay was in the middle of putting a paperback book back into her purse.

Karen was about to ask what the book was when the house lights flicked off and on again. The play was about to resume.

"Yep, this play is going to take hours at this rate" was all Karen said before the house lights went off and the stage lights came back on.

* * *

Scene I-3: Mary has concerns (cont'd)

HENRY (cont'd)

I think we can have the plumbers build a constantly moving water system so that no flushing sounds would ever disturb the play. The water will just be softly running below each seat. We could even have a water recycling system built in, but my worry is that some patrons, once they get going with their number ones, will lose control of themselves and number two into the system. We need to have some sort of system that will handle the solid waste and send that to the sewer main.

MARY

I see you have put some thought into this. That's good. I still have concerns about the costs and the logistics of getting this all together. But this is a good start.

HENRY

I'll let you know what the plumbers say. If we can do all that and keep the costs reasonable, then perhaps this will work.

MARY

Maybe we could have some sort of electrical shock administered to anyone who number twos.

HENRY

Ha ha. No, that would not be good for business.

MARY

I was just kidding.

HENRY
(stands up.)
I'll call the plumbers to arrange a meeting for tomorrow, if they are available.

MARY
All right. Let's see how this goes.

(HENRY exits the stage. Once he is safely gone,
MARY shakes her head.)

MARY
Men, right? *Aaargh!*
(Picks up one of the seated patrons in the doll
diorama audience and looks at him angrily.)
I am sure women will appreciate our efforts, but the
men will never stand for it.
(Laughs.)
(Blackout. End scene.)

* * *

Karen and Kay turned their attention to what was happening
on stage.

Without pause, the play went into a second scene, located
at the edge of the stage, where an old, black landline phone sat
on an old, wooden cocktail table, and next to it stood a small,
uncomfortable, functional chair.

Henry sat down in the chair and squirmed a bit to make
himself more comfortable, which seemed an impossibility. He
dialed a number and waited for an answer. He began talking to
the contractor, explaining what was needed.

This conversation was fairly redundant. The audience already knew all the information that Henry gave the contractor,

so Karen wondered why the playwright bothered repeating the same ideas. Perhaps the playwright was making a comment on the redundancy of life. Or perhaps the comment was on the redundancy of theatrical performance, which, particularly during a long run with the same cast, could go far beyond a feeling of déjà vu and actually begin to feel like incarceration. Karen remembered that from her mother, Dolores, who had been active in community theatre for many years. One of Karen's mother's plays, a version of *Hellcab*, had run for almost two years, and Karen remembered her mother's grumbling about it over the breakfast table. Dolores said that the play was delightful, but that even delight became tiresome after a year of doing it every night. Karen wondered if that was why her father had walked out when Karen had been only a pre-teen. Perhaps Dolores had just tired of the delight of being married. Of course, Karen's father had been abusive, so perhaps the loss of delight had been a justified response to the abuse. The real problem had not been the loss of delight but instead had been the abuse. Karen decided to think about this more later, but for now, the play was still going on. But then the buzzer went off again.

Karen realized she hadn't been paying attention to the play at all. She'd been lost in her thoughts. She looked over at Kay and asked her what had happened.

"Oh, nothing, really. It was just Henry saying to the plumbing contractor the same things we already knew. This play is dragging, and not just because of the buzzers."

"Want to just leave?"

"No. I am funny that way. I need to stay until the end. I am one of those people who watches every movie from previews through the final credits. We paid good money for these tickets."

"Actually, I won them from the radio."

"Still, they have value. We need to extract our money's worth from the experience."

Karen scrunched up her face into a mock grimace to indicate to Kay that staying would be okay, albeit a bit painful. "I hope we don't lose anything from this *experience*," said Karen, resigning herself to the evening's torture. Maybe the solution Henry and Mary needed was to seat the audience in Judas chairs. Although that would be horrible torture, at least the audience would be fully attentive. However, the screams could be distracting, so that probably wouldn't work. Still, thinking about it made Karen smile.

Kay pulled her book out of her purse again.

"What are you reading?" asked Karen.

"It's a play by Halldór Laxness called *The Pigeon Banquet*."

"He won the Nobel, right?"

"Yes. He was a wonderful writer. He wrote in Icelandic, which people thought was nuts because it limited his audience. Most of his contemporary Icelandic playwrights wrote in Danish in order to get their work to the mainland."

"What's the play about?"

"It's about a guy whose business is so successful that he doesn't know what to do with all his money. So he decides to host a pigeon banquet. He ends up inviting something like every fifth name in the phone book because he says that the phone book is the only place where the rich and the poor stand side by side."

"That sounds amusing."

"It is quite funny. It's a much better play than this one."

"Well, maybe," said Karen, "But maybe this play has a few surprises up its sleeves. What if it is trying to lull us into stupor in order to then hit us when we're unwary?"

"You think playwrights really think that deeply?"

"I am sure of it. My mom used to complain about play-wrights who were so subtle that their plays' deeper meanings were completely lost on most of the public. She'd say that nothing short of a two-by-four across the forehead would make much of a dent on the average audience member."

"Well, that *would* be the Theatre of Cruelty, wouldn't it?"

"Hey, what do you think will happen if Mary's idea goes south?" Karen tried to seem genuinely interested.

"Maybe someone will sue her."

"Sewer? They don't even know her."

"Ha ha ha," said Kay, enunciating each "ha" separately and slowly.

"I hope this doesn't take forever. I still have to shop afterwards."

"Oh, where do you shop?"

"I stop whenever I get tired," said Karen. "I pass three different grocery stores between here and home."

"You walk?"

"Of course. I live here. I don't need to drive."

"Oh, gosh. I couldn't survive without a car. I live way out in the burbs. It takes me an hour to get in."

'Yeah." Karen paused. She wished she could say so much more, but Kay would never understand. "Cars are expensive. I figured if I moved into the city, I'd be able to take public transportation everywhere and not have to worry about parking. Parking in the city is absolutely insane. And parking lots charge a fortune for monthly permits."

"True. But I like to get away from it when I want and just retreat into my private corner."

"I do that, too. It's just my corner is a bit smaller. But it's filled with wonderful musicians and actors and painters and writers. I love moving among them. I couldn't possibly be that socially distanced."

Kay looked at Karen oddly. Kay tilted her head to the side like an owl, and turned her head sharply to the left. "We must be at

29

different stages in our lives."

"Oh, shoot," replied Karen. "The buzzer just went off again. I think we missed the whole scene."

"No big loss." So they sat through another bathroom break, but by then they had run out of topics to discuss. Kay returned to her Laxness. Karen, not having brought a book, closed her eyes and listened to the ambient sounds of the room. She was listening for any voice she recognized, which would give her a reason to get up and leave her companion's side. However, from the *loge* level, she could not hear what anyone else was saying unless they were yelling. But that was amusing in its own right. When Karen had gone to concerts as a young girl, she'd always managed to make her way to the front of the stage. Sitting in the *loge* seemed so foreign. It was for dignitaries, and she for sure was not one. She liked her own sort of anonymity. She didn't need to run away to find it. Indeed, she thought, it was far easier to hide in a crowd than to hide out in the middle of nowhere.

* * *

Watching the play, looking toward Kay, Karen said that she was beginning to wonder why Henry was not more supportive of Mary.

"Is he a sociopath?"

"Shh! The play is going on," Kay whispered back, though all she really cared about at that moment was her Laxness.

Karen lowered her voice to match. "A psychopath?"

"What?" asked Kay, turning her attention away from Laxness for a moment. "Maybe he's a telepath," she said.

"No!" insisted Karen. "I am sure he's a hiking path!"

Kay put away Laxness and looked at Karen the way a dog food vendor looks at a cat.

"When we get out of here, how about we find someplace that serves squab?" Kay said.

"I don't know about that, but I know a few places with exotic meats. Have you ever had camel meat?"

"No, but I have read about hump fat."

"That's used as cooking oil at this place."

"They have anything else?"

"Sure. Kangaroo. Python. Ostrich."

"I don't eat mammals anymore, but ostrich sounds interesting."

"They also have wild snipe."

"Snipe? I was a pledge at a sorority in college, and all us pledges were sent off on a hunt for snipe the first fall I was there."

"Ah, that must have been a different type of snipe."

"Well, we never found one."

"I am pretty sure that was the idea. Snipe hunts are an old practical joke."

"That explains their laughter when we returned empty-handed."

"Did you end up joining?"

"No. I figured that any social group that embarrasses pledges by hazing them this way was not worth joining."

"I'd have to agree with you on that," Karen said.

"Let's watch this play," said Kay. "We might as well since we're here anyway."

Both women returned their attention to Henry, who was explaining the contractor's work schedule to Mary.

Karen was bored. "Who cares about all this? The play needs to get on with it. There's too much redundant exposition."

"Yeah, you could say they've been pissing away their opportunities to develop something new and interesting in the play."

"Ha ha ha," replied Karen, parroting Kay's careful enunciation of each "ha." But Kay was right. The play was bogging down in repeated minutiae. Fortunately, the act soon ended, and the first intermission began. People got up from their seats and began milling around in the halls. A long line for the bathrooms formed inexplicably.

"I'm going to get a drink. Do you want anything, Kay?" asked Karen.

"No, I'll just read for a while. You go ahead." Kay pulled Laxness out of her purse again.

* * *

The drink line was almost as long as the bathroom line. Karen began to suspect that the two might be connected in some way. She saw Rayro in the hall. He looked like he was monitoring the progress of both lines. Karen approached him, and when she was close enough to be heard, she asked him, "Are you the official line monitor, Rayro?"

"Oh, hello, Ma'am. Yes, I suppose you could say that."

"Call me Karen. I do not like being called 'Ma'am.'"

"Sorry. I should have remembered that. Yes, I need to make sure the line keeps moving. If it stops, something may be wrong closer to the front, and that situation might need some amelioration."

"Oh, Rayro, what big words you have!"

Rayro smiled at the Little Red Riding Hood reference. "The better to communicate with you, my dear," he replied.

Karen hadn't been intentionally referencing the fairy tale at all, so Rayro's calling her "my dear" took her aback.

"Rayro, I am stuck with a friend who is not a very scintillating conversationalist, and all she's doing during these interminable bathroom breaks is read a book she brought with her. I need something to read, too. Do you know if the gift shop downstairs sells any reading material?"

"Sure they do. They have some popular magazines and books, like crossword puzzles, books of trivia, that sort of stuff. Exactly the sort of material people go to if the plays don't interest them enough."

"Thanks. That is helpful." Karen walked down the carpeted spiral staircase that led to the main floor. There she went to the gift shop, which was surprisingly empty. Perhaps the rest of the audience was finding the play more interesting than she was. She looked at the different magazines and books on display. She picked a news trivia pocket-sized paperback and paid for it and a roll of wintergreen Lifesavers for herself and then returned to her seat.

Kay was still engrossed in her Laxness, so Karen began reading her trivia book.

A story from the *Hawaiian Gazette*, dated January 22, 1868, said, "A youth in Texas procurred [sic] about a gallon of bees, which he secured in a handkerchief and carried to a camp meeting. After the service was over, and just when the happiness of many was culminating, he turned his winged messengers loose, which is said tended very much to demoralize the auditory."

Karen astral projected out of the theatre and into that camp meeting. She saw herself sitting in the pews and waiting for the service to end. She had worn the sharp down on the end of a pew pencil by drawing intricate maps of a fantasy world on the collection envelopes. Her drawings were her gift, but she doubted that they were received as such.

Kay wondered how the guy in the Laxness play could have more money than he'd know what to do with.

Karen looked for the bindle stick that the youth in Texas must have been carrying the gallon handkerchief of bees with. No way was he carrying it in his hand. That would be crazy.

"Hey, kid!" she called to him. "What's in the snot rag?"

That got his attention. The kid looked up, and she saw fifteen angers in his eyes. None of them were directed at her, though, so she figured she'd be able to talk to him.

"None of your bees' wax," he said, after which he snickered.

"How'd you get 'em all in the handkerchief?" she asked.

"I stunned them and then put them in with some long tweezers."

"That's what I figured."

"Who are you?"

"I'm just another excaudate storyteller."

"What?"

"Have you ever considered the etiquette of how to stand in an elevator?"

"What do you mean?"

That's when Karen knew she had him. She had the response ready. "I mean, if you get into a crowded elevator, do you just turn around and face the door and put your back to everyone? Isn't that rude, to just turn your back on everyone? But if you don't, you have to be there for them to all stare at, and I don't know about you, but there's no way I can do that without becoming super self-conscious."

"Lady, you're crazy," said the kid, who walked away and turned a corner, never to be seen or heard from again. But then who ever does hear from corners? They are not sentient beings.

Well, that was a statement filled with thoroughcity! Open the hatch, and head underground. There, straight ahead, you can see it. The place with the communal pension plan. It is famous world over. They decided they'd put all their money into a pot in the center of town, and then they'd wait. The last person left would win it all. But the problem was they began to have more births than deaths. Eventually so many people were alive that the pension became meaningless. No last person would ever come. The money was being paid into a counting room with a person standing in infinity left to count it.

That person turned to look at Karen, but Karen didn't notice. She was looking at a spot on the floor and wondered if it was chewing gum or part of the pattern.

Then she heard her mom's voice: "Be prudent and perseverant, Karen."

So Karen spit on top of the spot just to make it definitely unpleasant.

Will the great bury her reefer with her when she goes down into the ground, underground, under town, undertow toward two tutus, too, to toot May tall tales in a rhythm schism that becomes the prison? Isn't it nice and shiny?

"Ma'am, are you okay?" asked Rayro, concern furrowing his brow. Of course it was Rayro.

"Where's the kid?" asked Karen.

"What kid?" asked Rayro.

"The one with the bees," said Karen.

Rayro shrugged. He had no idea what she was talking about.

"How'd you get to this camp meeting?" she asked him.

"What camp meeting?"

"Never mind. You don't know." She walked away as enigmatically as possible, hoping that the confusion was a sufficient smokescreen to let her escape. Before she knew where she was going, she had walked outside in a stupor and stood outside the theatre on the sidewalk, bumming a smoke from a nicotine fiend.

A neverland friend, a friendly end, the friend who'll end you'll be butter fool.

"Ma'am, you seem a bit disoriented. Are you okay? Can I get you any help?"

Karen looked up, and it was damned Rayro again. What was

he doing here at the Chicago Auto Show in McCormick Place?

"Ma'am, we're going to have to ask you to leave. Do you need assistance? We can call someone to help you if you do."

Well, that was an obvious threat if Karen had ever heard one. Enough was enough. She flicked her cigarette at a passerby but missed. She was going to fix everything, so she went back in and hoped to find her seat again. On the way to her seat, while avoiding a stand of bees, she passed a giraffe, a bandicoot, and a colobus. She wondered why the theatre had photos of animals on the walls, but then she noticed that the theatre was selling the animals for profit. Of course,

or

Karen began to feel self-conscious about wearing her elegant green evening gown while standing outside in front of the theatre. And she remembered she'd forgotten her hatinator. That was unfortunate. She'd have to go right back in. Or not. Here was Rayro.

"Ma'am, you forgot your hat." He held it out to her.

"*Hatinator*," she said, taking it from him. "Thanks." She turned away. That was all he really deserved.

But just then people began to run out of the theatre while screaming about bees. Ah, the kid got it done.

Her cab pulled up, so she got in. She asked the cabbie to wait for a minute in case Kay was coming out.

"Lady, I don't have time to wait. The police clear us out of these pick-up zones pronto. Your friend will have to get another cab."

"Oh, I guess you're right," said Karen. "Let's go."

And off they went, leaving the Pissers' Theatre and Kay and Rayro and everything behind. Kay wouldn't even notice until the end of the next chapter in her book, unless the bees got to her. And who the hell is Rayro, anyway? He's one weird usher. Karen was fine by herself, so good bye to them. That had been annoying,

or

Karen, sullen, rode home in the cab in silence, got out, paid the cabbie, and went up to her apartment. She had to *close the day on this one*. Something a boss of hers had once said.

Inside, a drink. A drink. If ever a day needed a drink.

She remembered the play, and then realized she had to pee. Of course. Pavlov. Ah, sometimes she hated knowing what she knew. Then she realized that what she really hated was knowing that she hated knowing what she knew. Hated growing what she grew. Hated flowing what she flew. Hated stowing all that stew in the trunk of her car. It was unfit for human consumption, so Pavlov was having her bring it out to the desert to give it to some dingoes.

At the sound of the bell the dingoes all pirouetted in unison, as trained, so that they might be able to eat. Karen was on a mission to save all the dingoes of Illinois,

or,

not.

Dingoes have gotten a bad name unfairly.

I've never even met a dingo.

I'm not even sure I've ever seen them at a distance.

So for me to say anything about them, like the fact that they are drug-addled lunatics who like to encircle what they are about to pee on, would be completely unfair.

I'll just shrug.

Shruggedy shrug.

Shruggedy shruggedy shruggedy shrug.

Karen's gotta carom off that bank, off the four into the two. That's what she's gotta do.

Sank it! Beautiful!

Okay, let's get out of here. This is not a friendly place.

ECKHARD GERDES

And we took our winnings and got the fuck out of there as fucking fast as we fucking could! We were so scared that we left a trail of shit. No shit.

Well, *that's not appropriate for the Pissers' Theatre*, I can almost hear them say.

Oh, well. Someone's always going to complain about something. I wish we could locate that someone and help them complain about what really needs complaining about, though. Some bones need to be picked…,

so Karen fell asleep.

* * *

When Kay finished her Laxness, she put down the book and looked blankly out at the dimly lit stage that might have been mid-scene. She wasn't sure. She hadn't been paying attention. But she quickly realized that Karen was gone. Had Karen said she was leaving? Kay couldn't remember, and the one image she'd had, of a pigeon feast, flew from her mind.

She found the valet, and he took forever to retrieve her Rav4™. She took out her wallet and gave him five dollars. She did not like overpaying for mediocre service, but she did so far too frequently.

When she got home, at first she was very quiet so she'd not wake anyone else up. But then she remembered that her mercurial husband had disappeared, again, and that her kids were all off at college or at work. She had nothing to concern herself over. And that might have worried her if she weren't happy to have some time to herself at long last. She set a bottle of champagne that was already chilled into the freezer in order to maximize its frostiness. Her favorite was when the water in the champagne began to crystalize. At that point the alcohol made its statement.

Two good old boys were on TV in a movie. One said to the

other, "My recurring dream has ended. I have always had this recurring dream of being lost and left out. This last time, I was lost but came to a restaurant, which I found was the destination for an entire class reunion that afternoon. Only six or seven people were there, so I pretended to be one of them. Was that wrong?"

The other shrugged and said, "Dunno."

"Well, you're no help," said the one.

"Welcome," said the other, obviously not paying attention.

She changed the channel. An old science fiction film was on.

"So you think you have me trapped, Hyperion? Well, you don't. I have built a death ray that will destroy the Earth!" The villain pulled the drape off his giant death ray contraption.

"I don't think you can, Trouncer. You forgot one detail."

"What are you saying?"

"How can you destroy the Earth with a death ray when the ray itself is on Earth?"

Trouncer looked chagrinned.

Kay changed the channel again, this time to a home and garden show.

A bearded man in a lumberjack shirt held a baseball bat as he stood in front of a tree.

"The avocado tree will not bear fruit until it is distressed. This is how I distress my trees." He took the bat and began beating the tree with it.

Kay muted the television. She went to the kitchen for the champagne. It was cold enough, and she didn't want to wait anymore. She opened the bottle and poured herself a flute.

Returning to the television, she changed the channel again. This time she found a cartoon she didn't recognize: "Tales of the Most Adventurous Chicken of All Time, Marco Pollo." Although it was a lame cartoon, it did not make her have to think at all, so she left it on and stared at it blankly, barely noticing what was happening in the show. She drifted off into sleep on thoughts of the pigeon banquet and Karen's disappearance.

As she drifted off, she felt a pang of remorse that she hadn't really paid attention to the play she'd paid to see. She decided she would go again later that week to see the rest of the play. And she'd call Karen in the morning to see if she'd come along. Kay would promise not to bring a book this time. She thought that perhaps her reading so much during the play may have been what put Karen off.

* * *

Two weeks later, Kay and Karen returned to the Pissers' Theatre. At first Karen hadn't wanted to go, but Kay apologized for reading during the play and promised to leave her books at home. She had begun reading Arno Schmidt's *Bottom's Dream*, anyway, and that was an eleven-by-fourteen-inch, fifteen-hundred-page monster of a book that weighed almost thirteen pounds. She would not have been able to fit that into her purse anyway, and she would have felt odd bringing a large-enough briefcase or messenger bag to the theatre. So with that assurance, Karen consented.

The women decided to meet for dinner before the play. Kay selected a restaurant she'd heard about in Greektown, not far from "Circle Campus," as she called the University of Illinois of Chicago, although the campus had changed its name in 1982. But Kay liked to hold on to old traditions, and once something had a name, she always referred to it by that name. The Willis Tower was still the Sears Tower. The Aon Center was still Big Stan. The Smurfit-Stone Building was still the Associates Building. Macy's was still Marshall Field's. Stroger Hospital was still Cook County Hospital. No way was Kay going to acknowledge the changes.

That would interfere with her general worldview, which was rather conservative in all but politics. Although she lived well off the money left to her by her corporate-shill grandfather, she always took a political stance against the corporate world. The contradiction eluded her, and when Karen had tried to point it out, Kay looked completely annoyed by what Karen was saying. Kay did not see any contradictions within herself at all, and no corrective lens could cure her myopia on the subject.

At least the Greek Islands restaurant was still the Greek Islands.

"Ooh," said Kay, looking at a fire at a table near where they were seated. "I am going to have that flaming saganaki, too."

"Oh, please don't. It's so embarrassing."

"What?"

"You know, it's not genuinely Greek. The guy who ran the Parthenon Restaurant like a block south of here invented it, and it's become a really touristy thing."

"Maybe we should go there instead."

"It isn't there anymore. It went out of business a couple of years ago. I think there's a sports bar there now. Do you want sports bar and grill food?"

"No. I wanted Greek. Well, okay. I won't embarrass you. I'll have the grilled calamari instead. Roditis?"

"Sure, but I also like retsina."

"Yikes. That stuff is bitter."

"Of course it is. It has pine resin in it."

"What? Why? That sounds disgusting." Kay made a sour face.

"The story I heard once from a waiter was that the Greeks used to make only roditis, which is delicious. When the Romans came marauding, they discovered roditis and loved it so much that they came back annually, raping, pillaging, and stealing all the barrels of roditis. The Greeks had an idea. They developed

41

retsina *because* it was nasty. When they saw the Roman ships returning, they took all the roditis and hid it in caves that the Romans did not know about, so when the Romans arrived and began drinking the wine, all they had was retsina, which they hated. The Greeks told them their grape crops had failed and that this was all they had. So the Romans left and did not return. But then the grape crops actually did fail, and all the Greeks had were the barrels of retsina. So they had nothing to drink but retsina themselves. After a while, they actually developed a taste for it, so they continued to make it."

"That sounds like a fake story to me. I think the waiter was pulling your leg." Just then the waiter arrived, so Kay dropped it. She didn't want to be criticizing waiters in front of a waiter.

"Good evening, ladies," said the young man who came to attend to them. "May I order you drinks before the meal?"

"Oh, yes, please," said Karen, taking the initiative. "We would like a bottle of roditis. And we'd like some appetizers. An order of dolmades. We can share them."

"And an order of calamari, too," added Kay.

"Wonderful. Would you like to order your entrées as well?"

"Well, you've eaten here more than I have, Karen. What is really good?'

Karen looked at the menu for a few seconds and then said, "I really like the Arni Aginarato. I would like that."

"What's that?" asked Kay.

"Lamb with artichoke hearts covered with a lemon-egg sauce," responded Karen, not giving the waiter a chance to go into his explanation.

"Ooh, I'll have that."

"Me, too."

"Two Arni Aginarato. Wonderful. I will have your wine for you in just a few minutes. Thank you." The waiter left, and Karen and Kay relaxed into a conversation about the changes in the neighborhood. Karen began to explain how the casino and the recent addition of a Five Guys burger place had affected the neighborhood's ambience. She said it didn't really seem like the old Greektown anymore. Kay replied that she hated change in general and was about to go into her standard spiel about social change in general when another nearby table had a saganaki blaze up, accompanied by the requisite shout of "Opa!"

"Tourists!" muttered Kay, with disdain in her voice, forgetting that she herself was just a tourist from the suburbs. Karen smiled at the thought that Kay was a walking bundle of contradictions. That's why she liked Kay. Kay was amusing.

After a few glasses of roditis, Kay began to talk about her woes with her estranged husband and his philandering, all of which bored Karen completely. Karen had long ago decided she was never going to marry and become a suburban wife like Kay. Hearing Kay's complaints reinforced that decision. Actually, Karen had no real interest in romantic entanglements whatsoever. She hadn't felt any sexual attraction to anyone for so long that she was fairly convinced that she was asexual, but even that wasn't anything she was really interested in thinking about. Other than hanging out with Kay from time to time, Karen preferred to keep to herself. She liked staying home in her apartment, reading, listening to music, and secretly making colored ink drawings that she would never show to anyone. She'd have some cannabis edibles and then sit down in front of her art paper with her many bottles of colored inks and her nibs. And then she'd begin applying ink to the paper. She put down a puddle of the ink and then pull it with the nib into lines and designs. She called it "playing in puddles," and it gave her more joy than anything else she did. But she had no formal art training and was very self-conscious about ever showing her work to anyone. She'd never even mentioned it to anyone, especially not to Karen, who was quick to judge everything.

"Well, I'm glad we didn't dress to the nines for the play tonight," said Kay, interrupting Karen's revelry.

"Well, that was for the premiere. Even then, did you notice how few people did actually dress up, even for that?"

"True. People just don't take these things as seriously as they once did. Jacob always used to blame the invention of blue jeans for the downfall of Western civilization."

Karen laughed heartily. "Oh, my god. That is really funny," she said between bouts of laughter.

"Well, maybe he has a point. But I am sure dressing up helped us get those loge seats."

"I am not so sure. But I did get us the same loge seats this time. I liked that area of the theatre."

"I did, too. And that young man you were talking to, what was his name?"

"Rayro?"

"Yes, Rayro. He was quite cute. Maybe he'll be there again tonight. You seemed to hit it off well."

Karen cringed. "No, thank you, Kay. He seemed nice, but he's really not my type."

"Because he's a foreigner?"

"No! That has nothing to do with it. Look, I really don't want to talk about that. Oh, here's the waiter. We still have time before the show. Would you like some dessert?"

"You are changing the subject, Karen."

"Yes, I am. You know, let's skip the dessert. I think I'd like an after-dinner aperitif."

"Here?"

"No, let's stop at one of the nice hotel bars nearer the theatre. Are you in the mood for a walk, or should we call a cab?"

"Walk? My gosh, Karen, the theatre is blocks away."

"Oh, sheesh. You suburbanites drive everywhere. I forgot."

"Well, we don't have sidewalks."

The waiter came over, asked if they wanted anything else, and Kay asked for the check.

"You got the tickets," said Kay, "so I'll get dinner."

"Thanks, Kay. That's nice of you. I'll go ahead and call for a Lyft while you do that. I just need to go to the washroom first."

"You'll have plenty of opportunity to do that at the play," say Kay with a short laugh.

"Ha ha! I'll never make it there. This wine has made its presence known." Karen walked off, and Kay began to look through her purse for her wallet. She couldn't find it, and that worried her. She'd bought her Metra train ticket online, and she'd used her credit card for that. She must have left her wallet on the desk when she'd gotten the tickets on the computer. But she had her phone with her, so she could use her pay app and pay for dinner that way. She just hoped that her wallet was actually at home. If not, she'd have a chore and a half cancelling all her credit cards that were in the wallet. She checked to see if any charges were pending on her major cards, but nothing showed up other than her actual purchases. She'd bought some CDs through Discogs and had paid for groceries, but nothing else was outstanding. *Outstanding.* What an interesting word.

The waiter came back with the bill. She asked him, "You do accept the PayApp, don't you?"

"Certainly, Ma'am," he replied. He pulled a scanner out of his apron. She opened the app to the QR code, and he scanned it. He gave her the scanner to sign and to add a tip on, and then he asked her if she wanted a physical receipt?

"Yes, please," she replied, handing him back the scanner after having added a twenty percent tip. He printed the receipt right from the scanner, tore it off, and handed it to her.

"Thank you, Ma'am. Please come again."

"We will," she said, not knowing if that was true or not. Karen returned and told her a car was on the way. It was still a half mile away, though, so it might be a couple of minutes.

"No problem," said Kay. "Let's wait outside." The evening was pleasant, so the wait was not a hardship, and Kay wanted to make sure they did not miss the car. Karen said they were looking for a 2019 Lexus LS.

"I don't know that car," said Karen, "but the picture shows it has a rather distinctive front grill. It's rather hideous, actually."

"That's your opinion. No Lexus is hideous."

"You are showing your classism, Kay."

Kay did not respond. She saw the car turn the corner towards them, so she waved at it. It pulled right over, and she held the door open so that Karen could slide through to the other side. Kay didn't scooch over on car seats. She thought it less than dignified to do so. But Karen was a city girl. She could scooch. Karen knew that Kay was thinking that, but Karen didn't care and had accepted Kay's hautiness long before. In fact, Karen was so used to it that sometimes it didn't even register with her. What was it that she'd read in some book by Covey, that we all have areas of influence and areas of concern? She had no influence over Kay's mannerisms. Karen could point them out, but Kay didn't seem to hear Karen on the topic.

No one said much during the ride to the theatre, and they left the car without much ado. As they entered the theatre, Karen saw Rayro, and he saw her. He smiled as they walked towards the stairs to the loge.

"Good evening, ladies. So nice to see you again. No hats tonight?"

"I was wearing a *hatinator* last time, Rayro. I've told you that

46

a couple of times!" said Karen with false exclamation.

"Ha ha! Yes, of course. The famous hatinator. That would be a good title for another play. Karen, correct?"

"My, you have a good memory. Yes, that might be a very interesting play indeed."

"Well, I hope you two enjoy the show. You must have enjoyed the opening night to return."

"Oh, yes, yes, we did. Thank you, Rayro."

"Thank you, Miss Karen."

"Please, just Karen. I am not a plantation owner."

"I'm sorry?"

"Miss Karen sounds like something from a Tennessee Williams play. I am from Chicago. *I am no Southern belle*," she said, drawling the last words in a very exaggerated Southern accent. Kay chuckled.

"Oh, I do beg your pardon." Rayro looked like he was worried he'd offended Karen.

"No problem at all. Have a good evening yourself, Rayro."

"Thank you, Karen. I hope to." Karen and Kay ascended the stairs to their seats in the loge. The theatre was only half as full as it had been on opening night. What a shame, thought Karen.

"Where is everyone?" asked Karen.

"They may be staying away because of the storm."

"What storm?"

"Oh, you didn't hear the storm advisory?"

"No."

"A big storm is brewing. There's a tornado watch. The storm should hit about when the play would normally be ending."

"What's normal for this play?"

"That's true. If it comes, it'll probably hit while we're still inside. But that's life in the big city, right?"

"I'm pretty sure storms hit everywhere."

"Ah, so you would think. But some places seem immune. When is the last time a tornado hit Chicago?"

"One hit the Loyola campus a few years ago."

"But they are rare. The lake winds repel tornadoes."

"Is that why?"

"According to Tom Skilling."

"Aha! Well, then it *must* be true."

"Ha ha. Sarcasm is so very unbecoming," said Kay. "And he actually *would* know. He's the best meteorologist in the city."

"Oh, Kay. You are wrong about sarcasm. It *is* becoming more and more."

"Ha ha. Well, let's hope for the best for tonight."

"I'm sure we'll be all right."

The house lights flicked off and back on.

✷ ✷ ✷

Scene II-4: The plumbing has problems

(HENRY and MARY are in the theatre box office, sitting opposite each other at the desk.)

HENRY

Oh, gosh. The bill from the plumber is due.

(HENRY holds up an invoice, waves it in the air, and then slaps it back down onto the desk.)

If we'd built the toilets to handle solid as well as liquid waste, this problem wouldn't have happened.

MARY

Well, we should have figured that some folks wouldn't be able to do one without the other.

HENRY

I still think that the idea to only accept liquid
is a good one. Otherwise the stench will be
overwhelming.

MARY

(picks up the invoice and looks at it. She sets it back down.)
Well, the plumber's idea of having a grate installed
in the seats is a bit draconian, but perhaps necessary.
That should discourage them.

HENRY

True. If they number two it, they'll have to sit on it.
But that may not stop the completely befuddled. We
can add signs to the seating stalls, and even then,
some of them will probably forget themselves.

MARY

So we need a backup plan.

HENRY

What if we added sensors and censers? The first will
alert us to the mishap. The second will release a local
aromatic that will override the odor.

MARY

Some folks are very sensitive to incense. But some
sort of air freshener would be good. We should also
look into adding localized air conditioning jets that
go off when the sensor is triggered.

HENRY

Yes. That could contain the air freshener. When a
patron triggers the sensor, air jets that release the
freshener are automatically turned on.

MARY

And an employee could then go to attend to the patron. We'll need to hire registered nurses for the job.

HENRY

That won't be cheap. We can't just hire high school kids for that.

MARY

True. We may have to raise ticket prices to be able to afford that.

HENRY

Maybe we could get some grant money. I'll look into that. It sounds like something the government might get behind in order to show they are doing something to benefit the elderly.

MARY

Good idea. Do that. We'll meet back up tomorrow. I'll look into where we can hire the RNs while you check into the grant money.

(HENRY and MARY stand up and exit the office door and exit the stage. End scene.)

* * *

The house lights stayed off. Another scene was coming without any delay, which was very unusual for this play. Karen looked at Kay, who was as glassy-eyed as she was. This was not really very scintillating theatre. Karen hadn't been expecting anything like a large, trivial spectacle, but still she almost wished Kay had brought a book. Karen felt guilty that Kay had to endure such tedium just because Karen had insisted on no books being brought. Was this a version of Artaud's Theatre of Cruelty? The attention went back to the stage as the next scene began.

* * *

Scene II-5: The box office is burgled

(TWO THIEVES, who are two of the FOUR RANDOM AUDIENCE MEMBERS, enter the box office and begin rifling through the desk and the filing cabinets. THIEF ONE takes a tablecloth off of what had looked like a small table and discovers a safe.)

THIEF ONE

You know anything about safes?

THIEF TWO

A little. Did you try the handle?

THIEF ONE

No.

THIEF TWO

Well, try it.

THIEF ONE
(tries the handle)

It's locked.

THIEF TWO

Don't spin the dial. I worked at a store when I was a teenager, and we would always leave the combination done except for the last number so that we could get in and out quickly with the register trays. Maybe they do that here.

THIEF ONE

What direction should I spin the dial in?

THIEF TWO

Most of these simple safes are four-number combinations going right-left-right-left. So try turning the dial very slowly to the left. You should feel the tumbler click when you reach the right number.

THIEF ONE

Can you do it? I don't feel comfortable doing it.

THIEF TWO

Sheesh. Sure, I'll give it a spin.

THIEF ONE

Ha ha.

(THIEF TWO kneels in front of the safe and puts her hand on the dial. Just then a cell phone rings in THIEF ONE's pocket. The theme song from a popular musical is the ring tone. THIEF ONE fumbles in his pocket and pulls out his phone, quickly turning off the ring tone.)

THIEF TWO

(THIEF TWO turns her attention to THIEF ONE and looks annoyed)

What the hell is that?

THIEF ONE

It's from that musical about cats.

THIEF TWO

That's not what I mean. Why the hell is your cell phone on? How do you expect me to hear the tumbler with that shit playing?

THIEF ONE

It's not shit. It's a Broadway show tune.

THIEF TWO

Yuck. Turn that damned thing off!

THIEF ONE

I did.

THIEF TWO

No, not just the ring tone. Turn the whole phone off. Otherwise it'll just ring again.

THIEF ONE

(looks at his phone.)

It was a call from my boss. I need to call her back.

THIEF TWO

Not now, knucklehead. You can call her when we're safely out of here.

THIEF ONE

Haha! *Safely*! I get it.

THIEF TWO

Shhh! Let me do this.

THIEF ONE

Okay, okay. What a grouch!

(THIEF TWO turns her attention back to the safe. She slowly turns the dial, and it clicks into place. She turns the handle, and opens.)

THIEF TWO

I was right. They had everything but the last number already dialed.

(pulls the door open.)

Crap! There's no money in here at all.

THIEF ONE

What's in it?

THIEF TWO

Bills, invoices, junk like that.

(pulls out some papers.)

Wow, they have some huge bills. This play couldn't possibly be making them any money. But their plumber seems to be getting rich.

THIEF ONE

What? Nothing of value?

THIEF TWO

Nothing at all. Wait. Here's something. This is weird.

THIEF ONE

What is it?

THIEF TWO

It looks like a handwritten manuscript of a novel.

THIEF ONE

Well, that's probably worthless. Who reads novels anymore? Who's the author?

THIEF TWO

I don't know. No author name is on it.

THIEF ONE

Well, that sure isn't the payday we were expecting.

THIEF TWO

Maybe not, but maybe this is a manuscript by a famous writer. We should look into it. I think it must be something, or why lock it all in a safe?

THIEF ONE

Maybe one of the theatre owners fancies themself a great literary artist.

THIEF TWO

The paper is far too old looking for that. And this has been written in real ink. Maybe it's the great lost manuscript of J. Meade Falkner's fourth novel. Or something else equally as rare.

THIEF ONE

What? Who was that?

THIEF TWO

He was a famous novelist in the early 20th century. He lost the manuscript on a train to Newcastle.

THIEF ONE

I thought you were supposed to bring coals to Newcastle. And owls to Athens.

THIEF TWO

No, you are not supposed to do that because coals come from Newcastle, and owls were already plentiful in Athens. So you'd be doing something superfluous.

THIEF ONE

Ooh, aren't we sophisticated? *Superfluous.* Pretentious much?

THIEF TWO

Using vocabulary well is not pretentious. Anyway, Falkner worked as a weapons manufacturer, and some people think the manuscript must have been stolen by an enemy agent on the train who thought they were company secrets.

THIEF ONE

Well, I doubt that this is what this is.

THIEF TWO

This is always what this is. That's what those words mean.

THIEF ONE

Oh, shut up. Let's get out of here. We need to find someone who knows more about literary manuscripts.

THIEF TWO

I know someone.

THIEF ONE

Of course you do.

(THIEF ONE and THIEF TWO leave the stage, exiting though the door stealthily.)

* * *

The buzzer went off again, so the house lights came back on. The audience tonight was letting the actors finish their scenes. That was polite.

Kay and Karen looked at each other.

Kay said, "Well, that was an interesting direction to take the play in, don't you think?" Karen replied, "Yes. Finally something is happening. But how in the world could a manuscript that got lost *en route* to Newcastle arrive in Chicago?"

"Maybe Jack the Ripper brought the manuscript with him to Chicago?" offered Kay, smiling.

"That wouldn't make sense time-wise. The Jack the Ripper killings happened at the end of the 19th century."

"Well, it could have been someone else. People must have

traveled from Newcastle to Chicago with some regularity in the early 20th century."

"Oh, maybe you're right. I read that British trade unions encouraged artisans to move to Chicago in particular because of there being too many artisans in England, which kept artisan wages too low. They wanted to reduce the amount of artisans in order to drive up their value. But that was also at the end of the 19th century," said Karen.

"How do you know all this?"

"I just finished a book on the fin de siècle, and it's still pretty fresh in the mind."

"Well, the manuscript could have taken a circuitous route and not come directly from Newcastle."

"True. Maybe the manuscript ended up in the hands of some Jewish people who loved literature and who came to Chicago to escape the horrible Russian pogroms of the 1920s. I think a lot of people were also fleeing Germany to escape that horrid Kaiser Wilhelm II."

"That's true. Thousands of Germans came over and traveled up the Mississippi and ended up in the Quad Cities. I met a pastor from Davenport at a dinner party once, and he explained all that to me. There was a waystation for German immigrants in Davenport, and from there they traveled throughout the Midwest."

"Oh, yeah. I read about that, too," said Karen. "I think that's why so many northern Germans gravitated to Wisconsin. Its rolling fields and climate were similar to home. That's why Wisconsin has so many dairy farms and Holstein cows."

"Oh, the Frisians, especially. Yeah, the pastor talked about them. He said his family had come from Jever, which is how he came to the Midwest himself."

Kay and Karen's conversation lapsed in silence because they were content that they had figured something out. Karen took a bag of turkey jerky out of her purse and shared it with Kay, and then both women ruminated.

* * *

Scene II-5: The box office burglary is discovered

(HENRY and MARY enter through the box office door. They see the safe uncovered and wide open.)

MARY

Oh, no! We've been robbed!

HENRY

Oh, no! But Mary, it's not as bad as it could have been, right? There couldn't have been much money. The theatre is almost completely broke.

MARY

That's not the problem. My grandfather's book was in the safe. I kept it there so that I wouldn't lose it.

HENRY

Your grandfather's book? He published a book?

MARY

No, it was never published. But this was the handwritten manuscript of it. I was going to try to have it published.

HENRY

What kind of a book was it?

MARY

It was a kind of Victorian novel with ghosts and séances. It was a murder mystery. It is actually not half bad. I was going to type it up and do some editing to it and send it to my friend Josiah at Farthing Stress Books in New York.

HENRY

Then don't bother editing it. Their books aren't very good.

MARY

What do you mean? They've published National Book Award winners, Pulitzer Prize winners, and even a Nobel Prize winner.

HENRY

That was back when they were independent. They are part of a huge conglomerate now, and all they care about are sales. I had a friend whose books were published by them, and he showed me one of his manuscripts. It was horrible. It had misspelled words and grammatical mistakes on every page. I asked him how he could justify submitting a book to them that was so shabby, and he just said, "That's what editors are for." But they published him anyway.

MARY

That is shocking. Why did they publish him?

HENRY

He was classmate of one the editor's daughters. He schmoozed his way in. That's the way most of them do it nowadays.

MARY

Well, then maybe my friendship with Josiah would help. But now the book is gone!

HENRY

Don't you have another copy? Didn't you Xerox it?

MARY

I was meaning to, but with everything we've been doing for the theatre, I just never found the time.

HENRY

Gosh, Mary. That is terrible. Let's call the police. They might be able to find it.

MARY

Okay. Can you call them? I need to figure out how much money was stolen and if anything else is missing. We had some contracts and invoices in the safe, too, and everything is completely in disarray.

HENRY

Sure. We'll find the book. I am sure of it. What's anyone else going to do with it?

* * *

Again the buzzer went off, and Henry did not have a chance to make his call before the stage lights went off and the house lights came on. Mindy and Aloysius just shrugged at each other.

"Let's say we just skip the rest of this scene, Aloysius. It's all implied anyway."

"But this scene ends the act."

"I know, but let's just go on to the next one. The burglars at the book dealer's."

"I'm fine with that. Anything to get out of here before midnight would be great."

"Okay. I'll tell the stage manager what we're doing. I'll tell him you are in agreement with me, and I am sure he'll go ahead and get it done for us." Aloysius went off to the wings, spoke with a woman there briefly, and then the curtain fell to signify the end of the act.

* * *

"That was a short act, wasn't it?" said Kay.

"It's almost as if they just cut that scene short."

"Maybe that's not a bad idea, given the challenged bladders. I think I saw more than a dozen people get up at the buzzer."

"I have to go, too. That wine is calling to me."

"I'm good for now, but you go ahead. I am sure you won't be missing much."

"That's probably true, but the play is getting more interesting now. I'll try to get back quickly."

"Okay."

"I hope I don't run into Rayro, though. He'll talk my ear off." Karen got up and went into the hallway. She looked left and right and did not see Rayro. She was relieved. Well, almost relieved. She still had to make her way to the washroom. She was glad she had brought her flask in her purse. She needed a stiff snort. The line for the loge washroom was longer than on opening night. She figured that people from other levels were coming here just to use the nicer washroom. That seemed unfair, but it was exactly what she'd have done if she were them.

Just as her turn came, she heard Rayro's voice call to her, "Karen!" She went into the washroom without looking back. She had no interest in having a conversation with him, at least not then. In the washroom, the speakers in the ceiling were playing some music from an old musical, *South Pacific* she thought. "Bali Ha'i" was the song. It started with a major seventh followed by a minor second, which was really odd to her ears, but she was sure it was the third note that added the strangeness to the charm.

How odd to be in a theatre that has a washroom in which the

washrooms played music from the theatre. It was so circular. She went into a stall, closed the door and locked it. She put the lid of the toilet down and sat on it and then rummaged through her purse. She pulled out her half-pint flask of absinthe and had a giant gulp of the sweet green liquid. She remembered a line from Hemingway's "The Hills Like White Elephants," one of the few Hemingway stories she really loved, in which the girl says, "Everything tastes of licorice. Especially all the things you've waited so long for, like absinthe." That was so true. But she loved the feeling she got from the absinthe. She remembered first drinking it because she'd read that wormwood had hallucinogenic properties, but that turned out to be wrong. People were just getting too drunk because the drink tasted so good. But she could swear it made her feel different than other alcohol. She'd known a guy who'd routinely drunk double shots of tequila and gin mixed together because he swore that the buzz from tequila was one thing and the buzz from gin was another, but the combo worked together synergistically. She liked each separately, but the combination just didn't taste good to her. Then she'd discovered absinthe.

She slugged down a third of the flask, and it hit her right away. She shook her head and expelled a huge gasp of air, shaking her lips in the process, which reminded her of the TV horse Mr. Ed. That struck her as funny. She began to sing "A horse is a horse, of course, of course" in amusement, but she had a huge coughing fit right then, so she had to stop.

A woman from the next stall called out, "Are you all right, girl?"

She was startled, but replied quickly, "I'm fine. I'm just trying to survive this long play."

The woman responded, "It wouldn't be so long if they didn't have the three hundred breaks. They are really mollycoddling the old, aren't they?"

Karen replied, "I think that's the point."

"Yeah, you're probably right," said the woman, and that ended their conversation.

Karen wondered what the woman had expected when she'd decided to come to this play. Perhaps the woman was one of those poor, self-loathing incontinent souls who liked to mock everyone else like them. Karen had seen this tendency before in people. They wouldn't mock anyone else other than themselves, but they'd disguise it in the mocking of others.

Karen waited for the other woman to leave and then took another big gulp of absinthe and found her disposable vape pen of sativa and took a good seven-second drag on it. She held back the temptation to cough because she didn't want to draw attention to herself in case anyone else in the washroom had been listening to her conversation with the other woman.

She felt the buzz coming on, so she flushed the toilet superfluously and left the stall. She went to the sink and looked at herself in the mirror while she waited for the water to turn hotter. She thought she could almost recognize the woman in the mirror. She then washed her hands and face, which was refreshing. She turned off the sink and pulled some paper towels from the dispenser. As she dried her face and hands, she came to the realization that the play she was watching was not what it at first appeared to be. It was actually a metaphor for life. She had just about figured out all the tangential connections that established the metaphor when she was startled by a nudge by someone else at the sink.

"Oh, sorry," said a woman about twenty years Karen's senior. "I stumbled a little. I don't wear heels very often, but this is the theatre." And then the older woman looked Karen up and down disapprovingly because Karen was not dressed up for the theatre this time as she had been for the premiere. Karen gave the woman the blankest smile possible and turned her attention back to the mirror. Karen's eyes needed more depth, so she decided to apply some contour below her brow bones. She did this in small dashes rather than drawing a line, and then she used her small dome brush to retrace the contour. She ignored the stumbler's departure. Oh, the lights blinked off and on again. The play was about to resume. She wondered what would happen with the lost book. She peeked out of the washroom door, but saw Rayro standing in the hallway. She closed the door again and decided to weigh her options before heading back out there. She decided what would be best was if she left the washroom the same moment several other women were leaving. That way she could use them as blockers and then peel off of them and head into the loge to her seat. There Rayro couldn't bother her. And Kay would be there to back her up that Rayro was being a creep when he followed Karen to her seat. She could file a complaint with the manager.

A trio of rather boisterous women, two dark-haired and one blonde, came in and kept talking in loud voices even when they separated into different stalls.

"I can't believe it," said the one in the middle.

'Can't believe what?" asked the one on the left.

"That he said he was going to resign. This morning he seemed okay." Apparently they were talking about someone at work. Good, thought Karen. Nothing she had to get involved in.

Karen pretended to be touching up her eyes when the women came out of the stalls and washed their hands. When she walked out with them, she kept to the side of them away from Rayro and then turned into the loge seating section. She would have to make her way from section to section through the seats, but that was better than a half hour conversation warding off Rayro.

Kay looked over when she saw Karen coming to the seats

from the other direction. Karen went through a row behind Kay so that Kay wouldn't have to be climbed over. Coming around from the usual side, Karen sat down.

"It's getting harder to avoid Rayro," explained Karen.

"I have no idea what you mean," said Kay, "but glad to see you back on time. The play's about to start back up."

Karen looked at the stage, but it began to look like a cross between *Vincent's Bedroom in Arles* and an Ames room, with its optical illusions. Had the set design changed, or was she just more sensitive to it after absinthe and sativa? She wasn't sure, but she liked the change.

The new act began with the burglars in the office of a book appraiser. He was looking at the manuscript with a jewelry loupe in his right eye. He pulled it away and looked up at the two thieves.

APPRAISER

It's old, all right. The ink and paper both place it somewhere at the beginning of the 20th century. And the style is quite familiar. I cannot quite place it. England, certainly.

THIEF TWO

We'd heard that it might be the missing J. Meade Falkner novel.

APPRAISER

Ooh, that would be quite the find. I assume you have no provenance for it.

THIEF TWO

No. That's why we came to you. I have a friend who has worked with you before.

APPRAISER

Well, I can't really say it isn't the Falkner novel. You

say it was in your family?

THIEF TWO

Yes, for many years. My great-grandfather was also
in the weapons trade. He and Falkner were friends
but also competitors.

APPRAISER

How would your great-grandfather have come by
this?

THIEF TWO

My guess is he was on the train with Falkner,
but Falkner got up and left the train before my
great-grandfather could. And then my great-grandfather found that Falkner had left the manuscript
behind. My great-grandfather grabbed it, intending
to reunite it with the author, but fell ill before he
could. He must have died with it in his possession,
and no one realized what the manuscript was.

APPRAISER

That's plausible. Let's go with that. Just write that up
and sign it, and I can go along with that. But I do
want a nice commission for this when I get it sold.
I think I may have a private collector who will be
interested. He actually has offices right in this building. I am sure he'll want the publication rights for
the book. We can argue that the rights were given to
your great-grandfather when Falkner made him a
gift of it.

THIEF ONE

That's not what happened, though.

APPRAISER

No, but it's better for the provenance. Don't mention that it was found. Mention that it was a gift. Perhaps it was a gesture of friendship. Or it was used to settle a professional debt? We'll come up with something. We will definitely be able to sell this, though. I am thinking six figures. I will want a third of it.

THIEF TWO

That is more than fair, right, Dusty?

THIEF ONE (a.k.a. DUSTY)

Seems that way.

APPRAISER

Okay, then. Dusty, Maggie, I will get to work on this right away. I should know something in a day or two.

THIEF TWO (a.k.a MAGGIE)

Thanks. Give us a call as soon as you find out anything.

APPRAISER

Will do.

(The APPRAISER stands up, shakes Maggie's and Dusty's hands. They exit the stage, and the APPRAISER begins looking through the manuscript in more detail. He picks up the phone and makes a call.)

APPRAISER (cont'd)
(talking into the phone)

Hello, Harold? Robert Aspidist here. I have something here you will definitely be interested in. Would you like to see what is perhaps the missing manuscript of J. Meade Falkner's fourth novel? Oh, you are? Great, I will see you in a few minutes.

> (The APPRAISER, Robert ASPIDIST, returns
> to his examination of the manuscript. The door
> opens, and the collector, HAROLD, walks in.)

HAROLD

Robert, thanks for the call. I came right away. Let me see that.

ASPIDIST

Sure, take a look.

> (ASPIDIST backs away from the book so that
> HAROLD can take a closer look. HAROLD
> walks to where ASPIDIST had been sitting and
> then sits down there himself. HAROLD begins
> looking at the manuscript with great interest,
> reading page after page.)

HAROLD

Interesting. Quite interesting. I see a few turns of phrase here that are definitely not Falkner's, but this seems to be written by a contemporary of his, someone of the same social standing.

ASPIDIST

Oh, well, that's a disappointment.

HAROLD

Maybe not. I think with a little editing to emend those stylistic idiosyncrasies and add some associated with Falkner, especially his rather odd use of commas and semicolons, we might be able to sell the manuscript to a publisher as Falkner's lost novel. We'll also have to change some of the dialogue here.

Falkner had his characters converse in speeches. This manuscript has too much back and forth in dialogue. But I can fix that. This is essentially exactly the sort of Victorian ghost story Falkner reveled in, so the foundation is there.

ASPIDIST

That sounds excellent.

HAROLD

Of course, I will want half the advance and half the royalties.

ASPIDIST

I have to cut in the actual owners of the manuscript, who want a third for themselves. I'd like to do a third, a third, and a third.

HAROLD

No, that won't work for me. I will be doing all the editing, so my cut has to be half. That'll still leave you sixteen and two-thirds, which will be a nice sum for just functioning as the agent here.

ASPIDIST

Okay, I'll agree because it's you. I trust you.

HAROLD

See? There *is* honor among thieves.

ASPIDIST

Haha! Very funny. But we're not thieves. We're just trying to fulfill literary dreams.

HAROLD

Ah, of course we are. We will be doing the world a great service by giving them an instant classic to read.

ASPIDIST

Exactly.

(HAROLD leaves with the manuscript. ASPI-
DIST picks up the telephone and calls MAGGIE
and DUSTY on the phone. They do not pick up,
so ASPIDIST hangs up).

ASPIDIST (cont'd)
(talking out loud to himself)
Well, I guess they're not back home yet. I'll try later.
(looks at the clock on the wall).
I need to get some food anyway.

(ASPIDIST picks his coat off the rack and puts
it on. Then he exits the room. The house lights
come up. End scene.)

* * *

Karen noticed how ornately carved the balustrade along the balcony seats was. The theatre wanted to give the impression that the
balcony was solid, but actually, two years earlier, Karen had been
in this very theatre for a jam band show, and the audience had
been dancing so hard that she could swear she saw the balcony
bouncing up and down, loose from its moorings, so to speak.
The balustrade did not fool her. The spot where she and Kay
were sitting was not beneath any balcony overhang. They were
tucked next to the reinforced projection room, which revealed
concessions made by the theatre in years gone by.

In the corner adjacent to the women's room, old candy bar
wrappers from the 1920s littered the floor. Charleston Chews,
Abba Zabas, and Oh Henry! bars were especially well represented.

They looked like they had been swept there into a pile a hundred years earlier. But the dust only looked a few days old, so someone seemed to be coming around to dust off the swept pile of candy bar wrappers. That seemed odd, but what else could possibly have explained it? Karen reached over to pick up some of the trash and throw it away into a proper receptacle, but she was stopped short by a clear acrylic coating encasing the pile of candy bars. When she looked closer, she saw that the entire pile was actually an art installation. How clever, she thought. But then she noticed one actual candy bar wrapper, a Baby Ruth wrapper, in fact, that had been added to the pile. It was not, at least at first glance, a part of the installation. Rather, what seemed to have happened is that someone must have passed the installation, judged it too hastily as a pile of trash, and contributed to the pile without realizing they'd just defaced a piece of public sculpture. Unless the extra wrapper had been placed there by the artist in order to see if anyone would pay close enough attention to notice.

Karen looked around and wondered how she'd wandered over here from her seat. She hadn't remembered getting up again. The weed. That must be it. Kay might be wondering what was wrong with Karen. Karen needed to go back to her seat and act normal for now. Yes. Or she could just fly free, roam around the theatre, flit about from here to there, watching Rayro try to keep up. She would elude him at every turn. There wasn't a person alive who could nail down Karen Zurück! Or Kay Cera, for that matter! Hey, where was Kay? When Karen returned to her seat, Kay was gone. Well, at least that was one less explanation to try to fake, she thought. Kay must have gone outside for some air or down to the gift shop. So Karen sat in her seat and looked at the darkened stage. She could see crew members moving scenery around in the dark, so she figured this would be the beginning of the last act. At last they had come this far! Only five hours had passed so far to get through four acts of the play. Logically, then, the play would only go for another hour and a quarter. So the entire play would last over six hours. Or would if everyone's bladders would only cooperate a little better.

∗ ∗ ∗

With so much wood piled up on the stage, a fire is being lit in the stove that heats Mary's apartment. Henry is lighting the stove.

Mary is sitting at the table. She is staring at a yellow pad of notepaper in front of her, pencil in hand. But she is not moving.

"Henry!" exclaims Mary. "People should judge us not by our words, but by our deeds."

"Now, you're just rushing to judgement yourself, aren't you, Mary? What if someone can't speak? Or is that being too embarrassed or something?"

∗ ∗ ∗

Karen was finding focusing somewhat difficult. Her attention to the play faded in and out, and she only caught bits of what was happening. Mary and Henry were at a loss about what to do. The play was not making money yet, though it eventually would once it had recouped the investment in the design of the theatre. And Falkner's novel, which wasn't really Falkner's novel, was being revised to look more like it could actually be Falkner's novel. No doubt Falkner scholars would come out of the woodwork and would try to discredit the book. They would cite Lee Israel and Araki Yasusada. They would say no one has the right to make money off of Falkner except those who have made a scholar's living doing so.

* * *

More wood is piled up on the stage. The fire in Mary's stove is burning nicely. She is sitting at the table and is writing on the yellow pad of notepaper that's there. She is using a pencil. At one point, she seems to be sketching. At another point, she is erasing something. At a third point, she is writing furiously, like a person possessed.

Henry stands up from his chair at the other side of the table, where he's been sipping his morning coffee while ostensibly looking at the newspaper. But he is much more captivated by Mary's mania. So with a disgruntled grunt, he shakes his head, folds up the paper and puts it back on the side table behind him, from which he grabs a different newspaper.

"Maybe this one won't be so damned blind," he says, going back to his seat and unfurling the new victim of his critical reading. Each day he scours the daily newspapers for warning signs of Libertarianism, which he feels strongly needs to be stomped out as quickly as possible, before it results in a return to the living standards of commoners in Dickensian London. He has a long speech at the ready about how Libertarianism in essence is Social Darwinism, which argues for the survival of the fittest. Society needs the weak to die in order to strengthen the herd. The cure for poverty is to let the poor die. The strong will survive, and the herd will be the better for it. And if the strong turn on the weak in order to cull their herd themselves, well so be it. That is the way of nature. This speech is one he has given a dozen times in his daydreams, but he knows he could never actually deliver it. He is no performer. He's a behind-the-scenes kind of guy. And Mary is pretty cool to work with usually. She's pretty well off. She's built a comfortable living for herself. And she likes to do things to help people of underserved communities, which is why she funded this theatre in the first place.

What Mary is sketching with such verve is beyond Henry's ability to guess. He has never noticed Mary engaging in visual art before. She isn't the kind to doodle during a conversation. This is new.

* * *

Karen noticed Kay coming back to her seat. Wow, that had taken a while. Karen just realized she hadn't been watching the play just now. She had been astral traveling through the scenes as if they were happening and she were there in person as an astral being. She had the ability to understand each character's thoughts and motivations, so she must be the omniscient narrator. She was God, or at least the God necessary for her to connect the play to her own world. It had a message for her.

Then her sarcastic superego interceded and broke the tension by telling her the message was a phony sense of wellbeing that overcame her when she was becoming deluded.

She had to be on her guard. Definitely she had to watch for Rayro. He was involved in all this somehow. She knew it. She looked back to Kay, who was only a few seats away now, and noticed Kay was not alone. She had Rayro with her! Oh, no! How could she?

"Hi, Karen," he called to her from halfway down the row still. The other audience members nearby hushed him and gave him evil glares.

"Look who I found wandering around," said Kay, in a much lower voice because she was closer. She went to pass in front of Karen in order to sit on Karen's other side, which would force Karen to sit between Kay and Rayro, if indeed he was coming to sit with them, which seemed odd anyway. Wasn't he working?

Karen pulled Kay down on the near side instead and whispered urgently, "Oh, sit here, Kay! I have missed you!" That way Karen would have Kay as a buffer between Rayro and herself. Karen took a pack of C. Howard violet mints out of her purse and put one into her mouth. The violet would mask the alcohol from the absinthe. Karen didn't want Rayro or Kay lecturing her. She offered a mint to Kay.

Kay shook her head and leaned to whisper in Karen's ear, "I hate those things."

Karen shrugged as if to say, "Your loss." But the play was going on, so neither woman continued talking. Both had expected Rayro to try to follow them to their seats. When Karen looked over to Rayro, he seemed to be standing in the aisle indecisively. But she couldn't tell if he was indecisive about his jeopardizing his job as an usher, or if he was just very timid. When she saw him look to her for permission to come over, she dismissed him with a wave. Seeing that she was not going to enter into conversation with him there, and that she was not going to follow him out into the hallway during the scene, Rayro retreated unobtrusively, probably to return to his neglected duties.

"At last," said Karen out loud, drawing hushes from neighbors and attention from Kay, who gave her a quizzical look with stern eyebrows, which was meant to convey both that she did not understand completely and that she thought that the subject was not serious enough to warrant conversation anyway.

Karen noticed this look of Kay's but chose to ignore it. She couldn't point out every time that Kay annoyed her without risking their friendship. Undoubtedly that was the same the other way around. But in the dark, when crickets rule, what piece of grass do you want to be on?

Kay and Karen left their seats, went to the washroom, and found a corner stall, the largest one. There Karen introduced Kay to vaping. Karen couldn't believe Kay had never run across it, but habits in the 'burbs are different from those in the city. Kay at first could only feel the grit in her teeth. But after ten minutes or so, she felt the grit dissolve into her jaw and then diffuse throughout her entire skeletal system until the viscosity of the body's fluids was kept stable.

Kay had never before had such an idea as the idea that grit dissolves differently for different people. Some don't seem to mind being dragged along through gravel as others do. In either case, dragging people through gravel is not the issue at stake here.

Karen was distracted by enormous *boinging* sounds. They were coming towards her from a silo by the side of the scythe that otherwise sang sweetly o'er the Salisbury Plain. This dysfunction, however, was put down to runic interference. Dissymbolism was beginning to dominate the arts once again. Nothing should mean anything. Everything simply is. Both the avant-garde, with its stance that art is at the forefront of our attack on the abyss, and the mimetic, with its claim that art imitates life, which, of course means it is but a reporter of what life is, miss the point. The avant-garde are worried with how art has to take us into new terrain, always, like expansionism under the guise of explora-tion. The mimetics, by following life around, put the concerns of life above the concerns of art. Their work may be first-rate political argument, highly astute sociological or psychological observation, or even a compendium of social effluvia, but it lags behind life.

And she had an image of someone flash before her: Knotso Badde, the lowest down varmint this side of the county line.

The wheels on the bus fall off and off, off and off, off and off....
Change the channel.
Catch yourself one hell of a buffalo down at Ted's Buffalo Ranch.
Find some music. Some random Krautrock channel is good.

Can. Neu. Guru Guru. Kraan. This is great. But the station is only playing the most obvious tracks from each.

"Hey, can I interest you in the purchase of some bedding made of the finest goose down? You will never sleep more comfortably."

"Where can you get it?"

"I heard 'Down by the Bay.'"

"Oh, you mean that wonderful old song by Curly Curve? Wow. I'd just about forgotten that."

"I remember I first heard them in a café in Berlin. The café was called something like 'The Drugge Shoppe,' which would have been hip at the time. They played great music. I stayed to listen. I remember I stayed a long time. I heard the Beatles' *Let It Be* and then Curly Curve. *The Forgotten Tapes* I think it is called now. It wasn't out yet at that time, but the manager was friends with one of the guys in the band. So he had the tapes long before they ever came out. Curly Curve was well known in Berlin, so the tapes were really well received. People came to the café just to hear the unreleased tapes of many musician friends of the manager. People were amazed that he could land so many big acts, but if they saw what he was handing to them along with payment, they wouldn't have been so shocked. That he was their dealer was no surprise. Even the name of his place thumbed his nose in the direction of the authorities. He was not surprised, nor was he concerned. Until he was busted. Then he found Jesus in a hurry. The script he was following was not a very fresh one. Not nearly as fresh as *The Pissers' Theatre*.

Karen looked over at Kay, who was bobbing to some song that was playing only in Kay's head. The people on stage looked like they were arguing again. Was Kay finding the music in the cadences of their argument? That would be wild. That reminded Karen of an interview she'd heard or read with Eric Belgum about his work. Belgum had discussed how his CD *Bad Marriage*

Mantra had come from an incident when he and his wife were listening through a Toronto hotel wall to an animated verbal fight in the next room. Belgum explained, "The argument had a great deal in common with many musical and literary traditions: the use of intense but slightly varied repetitions coupled with sparsely chosen materials. Play the CD as an installation piece at music and theater events, or at parties. Start it playing on the radio, then sit back and wait for the FCC to show up. Perform it as an instrumental piece with the instructions being simply, 'Use your instrument to censor the profanity.'"

Kay was still bouncing in her seat, happier than Karen could ever remember seeing her. The vape seemed to be good for Kay. Oh, Kay....

The term "block quotes" sprang to Karen's mind, but she had only an idea of what that meant. It was something from the deep recesses of the...

...secret lair of the...

...creature from the black spittoon! She'd gone to college at a small private college on the river. She'd shared a class with one of the school's starting baseball pitchers. This guy would bring in empty cola cans to spit his tobacco juice into. It was a small workshop class, and all semester long she had to watch this guy spit his cud into a can. She would feel like retching whenever she saw him do that and would have to spend some time staring out the window at the campus quad in order to steady herself again. The experience of college in general was something she wanted to leave behind.

Karen decided that she would someday start her own theatre company and make it all nonlinear and cochineal and corporeal and calcaneal and killdeer and sandpiper. Tobacco was not very popular anymore, not even in dipping tobacco form. Otherwise a Spitters' Theatre might have been a good sibling to the Pissers' Theatre.

When she looked down at the stage, she thought she was looking at the creature from the black lagoon....

...spittoon!...

...but when he turned to the side, she saw it was just Henry in the shadows. She was disappointed. That would have taken the play in an entirely different direction. She'd really lost track of the play.

As if reading Karen's thoughts, Kay said that she was sure that Mary's left ear hung a bit lower than her right one.

Karen noticed that Mary was wearing Mary Janes, so that made Karen wonder if Mary's middle name was Jane. She was wearing an item of clothing because it had her name. What would Jon Hamm wear? Would he wear pigskin in the bathroom? Was Jan Hammer more of a ham than Jon Hamm? Would Hamish Carter carry Karen's pork purchases home for her?

Kay let out a snort in coincidence with Karen's revelry on all subjects porcine. Karen looked over, wondering how Kay knew what she was thinking about, but it was obvious that Kay didn't. Kay was still lost in her own world. She was a lightweight.

Karen remembered something she'd seen at a Grateful Dead show years earlier. She'd seen one fellow who had found his space on the lawn, put down his little blanket, and proceeded to dance for every remaining minute of the evening. He danced through the intermissions. He was hearing music that no one else was hearing. Yet he danced. And not just passively shuffling his weight from foot to foot. No. He was twisting and turning, straightening and lowering his legs as fast as his heart beat. It was quite an impressive feat, actually.

Kay looked at Karen, and seeing a smiling friend, said, "The fact that you didn't thank me has made me thankful."

Karen had no idea what that meant. She thought that perhaps

Kay was saying that she had gotten something by not getting it, but that seemed to be some sort of contradiction. Of course, on another level, it made sense. She recalled that at school one of her girlfriends, one for whom everything seemed to come easy, for whom suffering was a few generations back, had said to her that nothing comes one's way until one stops wanting it. Karen had the feeling that she'd heard that in an old Allman Brothers song, but she wasn't sure. At any rate, Kay looked happy. The play was not so bad all of a sudden. Of course, she had no idea what was happening on the stage right then.

"Melissa" was happening. Of course she was. She was shimmying and shaking in zigzag patterns in front of Duane's guitar. Of course she was.

Kay leaned over again and said, "Good thing for the mask manufacturers that people have ears."

Karen let the words form a mandala that became fractals and replied, "You know you have to boil the shit out of chitterlings to make them edible."

She hadn't really heard Kay and was just saying whatever came to mind.

Kay didn't really hear Karen, either, and thought she heard something about Lady Chatterley and couldn't have cared less.

Instead, Kay yelled, "Do not pull over! Do not apply the break! Throw your license and registration out of the window while maintaining speed!"

"Don't laugh, Kay! I have a death ray pointed at the Earth from a really tall building!"

"Hey, I saw that gag in that old TV show *Chunky Blewster.*"

"I don't think that was its name."

"No, but it's funnier."

"Hey, I was told by someone that I should always ask any person I come across what they want. What do you want, Kay?"

Kay turned to look Karen in the eyes. Karen was such an interesting woman to her. She was free and in the city. She could move among interesting people, talk with strangers, of whom she made new friends every day. That was a beautiful world. Kay, however, was stuck. She'd never get out of her doldrums, and she'd never even shot an albatross. That just wasn't fair.

Albatross!

Oh, yeah, of course. Go for the obvious. She had no idea why she'd said it. But which *she* was which? No one knew for sure.

Karen knew. But she dismissed Kay's myopia as being a result of her upbringing and current living situation. Remaining relevant was rough when one was relegated to the suburbs.

"What do I want? In what sense? I want to go to a bar after the play. That's one thing I want."

"No, what do you *really* want?" Karen asked with her furrowed brow.

"Truth and beauty."

"You can't have them. Keats already claimed those. What else?"

Kay had nothing. She said so. "I have no idea what I really want. The thought never crossed my mind."

Karen looked up from her conversation with Kay and saw Rayro coming down the aisle towards them. He saw her see him, so he stopped and put his finger up to his lips in order to tell her that she and Kay needed to shut up. There was a play going on.

She nodded at him. She turned to Kay and whispered, "Rayro wants us to be quiet."

"Rayro?" whispered Kay back.

"Yeah, the usher. You remember."

"Oh, yeah. That guy." Kay put her finger to her lips and nodded to Karen.

Karen turned her attention back to the play. So did Kay.

81

* * *

They woke up when Rayro shook Kay's shoulder. Karen was out of reach.

"What?" Kay was disoriented.

"The theatre is closing. You will need to leave now." Rayro sounded very matter of fact about it. Kay detected no affection at all. Karen must be wrong about this guy. She shook Karen's knee.

Karen stirred. "Huh?"

"Sweetie, your boyfriend wants us to leave."

"He's not my boyfriend."

"I was being sarcastic."

"We missed it. What happened?"

"You could ask Rayro."

"Ha… ha… ha…."

"Well, now I'm determined. I've come all the way to the city to see this play twice, and both times I didn't see the whole thing. We are coming back. My treat. We have to see the rest of the play."

"Gosh."

And so it was decided.

* * *

When Karen and Kay stepped back onto the sidewalk, they decided to walk to an Irish pub a block away. Kay said she had a taste for a Guinness. Karen suddenly had the taste for one, too. The evening was getting late. The people on the sidewalks were having problems staying out of Karen's and Kay's zigzag ways. But they eventually wove their way through the groups of walkers until they came to an immovable object, an immovable feast, a stand of books for sale. They were arranged neatly in cartable wooden display boxes that had easel legs to keep the books displayed at a propitious angle. Kay couldn't help herself. She had to stop and look at the selection. They were unusual titles. Kay couldn't tell if they were proscribed political tracts or pornography. One, for example, was called *Mussolini's Little Girls*. It could be either. She wanted very much to pick it up and look at it, but just then Karen grabbed her by the shoulder and said, "Look! There's that guy from the theatre. Rayro. What the hell? Is he following us?"

Kay had been inebriated before. She wasn't going to trust the first thought that came to mind. She needed to give herself time to sort through the evidence. She looked over, and, sure enough, there was Rayro, coming towards them, eyes pointed right at them.

"Shit," said Kay, summoning forth all the profundity she felt capable of at that moment.

"Double shit," agreed Karen. "Let's get out of here. You know the Pedway system?"

"Yes, I've read about it."

"We'll lose him there. Come with me. We'll go in at Washington and State and come out at Randolph and Michigan. We can always lose him in Millenium Park." She grabbed Kay's hand and pulled it. She and Kay began running, still zigzagging, always zigzagging, hoping their patterns were impossible to follow. They went through a couple of buildings from one side to come out on the other until they were able to sneak into the Pedway entrance, pretty sure they'd not been noticed. Rayro was nowhere to be seen. But then Karen began to wonder if Rayro was even a threat. Had she just made up the threat in her mind? Maybe he was on the sidewalk because, hell, he was a Chicagoan who was on the streets of Chicago. Wow. How unusual. Kay and Karen happened across a Polynesian-themed bar in the Pedway, so they stopped there. Karen wanted a Mai Tai. Kay wanted a Mai Tai.

And Trader Vic's was no longer nearby. It had transported all the captured werewolves to London. Something like that. Warren Zevon knew. Maybe Rayro was an agent sent by Warren Zevon. That would be—no, that was crazy. Karen sat down at the first open table hard. She wanted to convey to anyone watching that she was not worth talking to. She wanted her distance respected. Even talking to Kay was becoming difficult. Karen was an INFP. That meant that she was okay with people, but they drained her. After a while, for Karen, people seemed like energy vampires. And because she was an INFP, they could not energize her in return. They would just drain her bloodless and leave her empty husk by the roadside. This was how every relationship had ended for her.

Karen shuddered at the thought. How many roadsides had she ended up alongside? She couldn't count them all. She was expected to magically know everything in life, and anything she didn't know was a deduction.

"Fuck!" yelled Karen, not knowing why.

"Is everything okay?" asked a young woman in a coral-colored waitstaff uniform.

Karen looked up at her. "Sorry," said Karen. "I just remembered that I've forgotten something."

"What'd you forget?" asked Kay.

"I'll tell you later, but most important things first—our drinks! We'd like two Mai Tais, please."

Kay, who had been looking at the menu, added, "Let's also get an appetizer. We'll split an order of mini shepherd's pies and an order of bacon cabbage dippers, please."

The server nodded and said, "I'll put the order in right away. I'll get your drinks in a minute." She left the menus because Kay and Karen should order more than appetizers.

"You got grace from me once. You shouldn't have expected

it twice."

They looked up in unison to see Rayro looking down on them from some moral high ground that only he knew about. Karen freaked out and ran out of the place screaming!

No, actually, she was still in line, waiting to pay for her cafeteria cuisine. The server was she! The server was herself? She was the server?

* * *

When we walk, we wind our ways towards worlds we had never envisioned. Whatever our fantasies had prepared us for was inevitably destroyed. I am sorry that I can't tell stories the way the others can. I try. But I fail. I ask for your forgiveness.

I have no idea of where we are. I had a rough idea of where we were going when we left, but the map was lost somewhere. But never fear! We'll find our way out of here!

* * *

Karen looked up again. She did not see Rayro. Had she really seen him at all? Did he even exist? What kept happening at the end of the play that lost Kay's and her attention? Or rather, what didn't happen? Had the play disintegrated into philosophical meanderings? Had it slid into lilting laments that lulled everyone unconscious?

She had a plate of food in front of her. Where had it come from? Had she ordered it? It looked like a couple of bacon cabbage dippers and a miniature shepherd's pie. How those miniature shepherds made pies so good, she'd never know. Boomchakalaka! She'd be here all week! Try the bacon cabbage!

She looked over at Kay's place at the table, but Kay was missing. Kay's food sat there untouched, but Kay had unfolded her napkin. She was probably just in the washroom. Or in the arcade playing a video game. Karen chuckled at the thought.

After a half hour, Karen became worried and went to the washroom to look in on Kay. Kay wasn't there. She must have left without eating. How odd. Karen finished her appetizers and had the server wrap up Kay's. Karen apologized to the server, but Karen and her friend would not be able to dine there after all. She thanked the server for the delicious appetizers, paid the bill, took Kay's leftovers, and went home. She'd call Kay in the morning and let her know the food was safe.

What could have happened? Perhaps the buzz had been a little too strong for Kay, so she'd decided to head home. The good thing about the commuter train that Kay took in and back from the suburbs was that her stop was the last one. She wouldn't miss it. Karen had a friend who'd fallen asleep on the El after having been at a wedding, and when he woke up, his shoes and tuxedo had been taken right off his body. One had to be careful, even on a suburban commuter train. Karen would call Kay in the morning. She was too tired to do it now. She just wanted to get some sleep.

She entered her building and walked up to the second floor, where her apartment was. She fumbled a little with the keys, but eventually found the right one and opened the door. She felt a wave of relief wash over her as she closed her door behind herself and then locked it. She tossed her keys into the bowl atop the teak shoe cabinet by the front door. She'd inherited the cabinet from her mother, who had what one could call a passion for shoes. Funny that the cabinet had come to Karen, who preferred being barefoot whenever possible. As Karen kicked off her shoes and put them away, she remembered how her mom would wear high heels around the house. Karen had asked her about that, but her mom just brushed the question aside and said, "One has to wear nice shoes, dear. People will judge you by your shoes."

Karen had decided at that moment that she never wanted people who judged people by their shoes to ever be in her life. She did not like those people. They were shallow. They were bigots. That's who people who judge others by appearance are. So she preferred her comfortable shoes, and all fashion be damned! She only wore flats and preferred her canvas sneakers to just about any other footwear other than being barefoot.

She went to the kitchen and pulled a bottle of white wine out of the fridge. She grabbed a glass, a wood block with cheese and a knife, a box of woven rye crackers, and she parked herself in her favorite chair in front of the television. She put the food and drink on the walnut side table next to her recliner, in which she often fell asleep because it was just that comfortable, and she turned on the comedy rerun station. What were Lucy and Ethel up to next?

* * *

In the morning, Karen tried calling Kay, but got no answer. Karen began to be a little concerned. Had Kay made it home okay? Karen wished she'd tried calling Kay the night before, but Karen had been too out of it to think about talking on the phone. She'd just trusted that Kay knew what Kay was doing. Perhaps that had not been a good assumption to make.

Karen turned on her TV. It was on the HBMX channel, which she'd never heard of. She figured it was for people who shot heroin and then did bicycle motocross. But she didn't know anything about either of those worlds. If indeed they were different.

She turned the channel. The next was a baseball game. She could tell the one team was the Yankees because everyone outside of New York hated them, but the other team she didn't recognize.

Its logo looked like it said "BM," which in her world meant "bowel movement," but why would anyone name themselves that? Obviously, something here did not make sense.

The next channel had Spirit doing an amazing version of Alan Toussaint's "Get out of My Life, Woman." That was great fun for a bit. She remembered the Leaves' '60s pop version, too, and was happy to hear this one. A good song should hold its own despite its many different treatments. Otherwise all one is judging is the performance, and that's another issue.

Kay still wasn't answering. That was unusual, but not alarming. Karen didn't know Kay to be much of a drinker, so maybe these were just the hangover horns playing on Kay. Karen remembered her mom's telling her that early in the morning in the "olden times," the first thing on TV was the farm report. Her mom told her that insomnia was such a burden that her mom would breathe a sigh of relief when the farm report came on because that meant she'd survived another night. In retrospect, that seemed quite a burden to lay on a child. But Karen's parents were not the kindest or most attentive a child had ever had. Nor did she think that her upbringing was much of a topic of conversation, so she'd never bring it up to anyone. Why should she? Who'd care, anyway?

Kay might, but where was she? Karen looked through the channel guide to see if anyone had a replay of the morning's farm report on. But none of her 187 channels seemed to. Farms were becoming obsolete. People were no longer eating food. They were feeding on right-wing propaganda-machine extruded pabulum.

Karen cracked up. She laughed because she could just imagine what Kay would say if Kay had heard Karen say that: "Pabulum? That is unfair to parents who need to feed their infants mushy cereal before any solid food can be introduced." Kay was amusing. Karen was sure that Kay was far more centrist than

Karen was, but Kay never went on rants about her beliefs. Karen could tolerate that, even if Kay's politics were way too suburban by Karen's standards. She'd remembered a story Kay had told her about Kay's father, Paul. Paul had been elected or selected or whatever to the local township library board. The town was building a new library. An argument ensued about installing a sprinkler system in the ceilings. Paul had made the argument that the cinderblock building would not be the valuable commodity at stake. The books would be. Water was just as much an enemy to paper as fire was. They were amazed! No one else had considered that! That, and the fact that the library was at least two hundred yards from any other building, obviated the need for sprinklers.

Karen rang again. Finally! Kay picked up and, quite slurrily, exhaled an exasperated expiration.

"Did you just die, Kay? Say something!" demanded Karen.

"Uh. Oh. I'm okay. Not feeling well. Gotta go. Sick. Bye!" and the phone call was not ended. Karen could hear the roars of Kay's ejections for quite a while.

When the challenges to all things quiet had calmed down, Karen softly said, "Are you okay, sweetie?" into the phone. She couldn't hear any sign that Kay was still alive. She listened close, but then the phone call timed out for some reason. Too much silence, maybe. So Karen called again.

After three rings, Kay picked up again and said, "What we need are some Yankee Clippers, I tell you," presumably referring to the game with the Bowel Movements the night before. Whatever that meant. Apparently the only detail that Kay remembered from the end of the evening was the baseball game.

"Game's up," said Karen. "How about you?"

"Karen, I'm sick," Kay said, and then sighed.

"You should get some chicken soup. Can you call the deli and have them bring you some soup?"

"Oh, some chicken soup would be amazing."

"Okay. I'll order it for you and have them deliver. I'll get you something good. Kreplach? Or is that too spicy? Matzo ball?"

"Oh, you know me. The kreplach would be great."

"Okay, I'll place the order. Keep your ears open for the delivery. Also, there's Alka-Seltzer in the cabinet next the sink, if you need. I left it there last time I was over."

"What?"

"I leave it everywhere I go so that I always have some nearby. Don't ask. It's an obsession. You don't need me to come out, do you?"

"Uh, no. Please, I just need to pass out."

"Okay. I'll have delivery leave the food by the carport, by the side door. That should keep it safe until you feel up to opening the door. Just in case you're asleep, I mean. At least the temperature is nice and cool, so nothing will go bad."

"Okay. I gotta go. Thanks, Karen. This is nice. You sure you're not a suburban mom?"

"Yeah, but I grew up with one."

"Me, too."

"I know. Talk to you later."

* * *

As Karen got ready for her and Kay's third attempt at surviving *The Pisser's Theatre*, she decided not to bring the vape. That had gotten a bit awkward. She decided a couple of edible gummies would work better. She was glad that she didn't have to drive. Kay would sometimes drive in from the 'burbs, and Karen always worried for her. But for the last few visits, Kay had been good and taken the train. Whenever Karen went out to Dunghole, as she called it, she'd take the train there. She had no reason to own a car. One could navigate the entire city with public transportation. And for the most part, public transportation was faster than driving, which could take forever because of the city traffic congestion. And even in Dunghole one could call for a ride share.

"It's not called 'Dunghole'!" Kay would exclaim when out of patience. But Karen figured that the one thing city folks had over 'burban folks is that they were close to the center, and they could lord their proximity to the heart over those who were farther away. Of course, that was predicated on the desire to *be* near the heart to begin with. For Karen, to be so far from the center was as good as being in a dung hole. And, besides, the name of the town Kay lived in sounded very close to "Dunghole." People had been calling it "Dunghole" for generations. People could be cruel with city names. Scumburg. Vermin Hills. She'd heard the horrible nicknames. She didn't use them herself, but she knew them. Did silence exonerate her from knowledge? She thought not!

＊ ＊ ＊

She thought not. That was how she felt at the moment. She was so incapable of thought that she couldn't even figure out how to figure out where she was or how she'd gotten there. Kay knew she was corporeal, but her tactility was failing her in both directions. She could not feel, not could she be felt. Not easily, at least. But she knew that she had to meet Karen at the Pissers' Theatre one more time. The third time would be the chum. Several weeks had passed since their previous attempt, and Kay had found the return to sobriety difficult after that. So she'd avoided it. She rekindled her fondness for gin and tonic, and she resolved to merely get by. But she had one last hope before collapsing back into the dull house. She wanted to understand what the twelve sardonic dreams were. She should have tried to stay sober to go see Karen, but Karen wasn't going to be sober, either, so there! Be there! Live in the present! Accept all bromides!

She liked Karen's cynicism. Kay saw herself in it. But that arm's-length stance was nothing new to either of them, nor to the families from whom they had come.

Kay slid a Pat Metheny recording into her car's compact disc player. A piece he did with Jaco Pastorius and Bob Moses. One of those amazing ECM recordings that helped her through her breakup from her first boyfriend, back when she was in high school. He had been a really nice guy. Not a great looker or any-thing, but he was kind. She'd gone with him to this small cof-feehouse, the Amazing Grace Coffeehouse, in Evanston, where they were going to school, and there they saw Metheny with the Gary Burton Quintet with Eberhard Weber, around the time of *Ring*. Hadn't that been Metheny's first national tour? He was so young. And so handsome. And so talented. "Bright Size Life." That's what it is. She liked the feeling she was having, and she even enjoyed the drive on the highway. The traffic wasn't too bad yet. It was early enough that rush hour hadn't started. She figured she should avoid as much traffic as she could, but she couldn't face another train ride. Some of the people on the train just scared her. But she had enough in the account to get down-town early, check into her hotel room, get in a quick swim in the pool, shower, get dressed, and be ready to meet Karen to try to see the rest of the play. They had no need to rush, though. They'd seen the start of the play a couple of times. They only needed to get there in time not to miss where they'd left off. Normally theatres wouldn't seat late-comers, but with the dozens of buzzer breaks, entry should be easy.

The Metheny was making her too sentimental. She took it out. She had loved the music at the time, but now it brought up regrets. She hated regrets. She needed something else.

Ah, she had Edgar Froese's wonderful *Aqua*. She could arrive in a condition of complete peacefulness if she listened to that. Karen would be amazed that Kay had not been fazed by the day's-worth of driving she'd spent to come into the city. But of course Karen, not even leaving the city, would not know what sort of distance the trip actually was.

She remembered one time when she was young some of her parents' European friends came to visit.

We were living in Evanston, outside of Chicago, and they asked us if we could take them on a daytrip to the Grand Canyon. They had no concept of the distances in America, or of the great degree to which too many people work too hard to increase those distances.

She'd written a poem back then. She remembered it verbatim:

We aren't in need of being able to enunciate with clarity in order to convey meaning.

We aren't in need of being able to speak clearly.

We aren't in need of being able to speak.

We aren't in need of being able.

We aren't in need of being.

We aren't in need.

We aren't in.

We aren't.

If that hadn't been a cry for help, then so help her, she didn't know what was. But she had been very young and ambitious. She'd gotten waylaid by a sour marriage, but that was over. But now she felt adrift. Her evenings with Karen were the highlights of her month. But other than these evenings, Kay felt like she was floating through life without a purpose.

She remembered Karen's question.

What do you want, Kay?

What *did* she want? What was she *supposed* to want? Why

were people expected to have specific *wants*, anyway?

Kay heard herself and began laughing. *Well, don't we sound pretentious?*

She pulled into a space that was miraculously open in front of Karen's apartment building. She had about four inches of room to maneuver in with, so it took some give and take, but once she had successfully parked in the space, she was proud of herself for it. She hadn't lived in the city for many years, but some things she couldn't forget. Parking was one of them.

She went into the lobby and scrolled down to the buzzer for Zurück. With a bit of trepidation, she pushed it. She had never been to Karen's place before.

And she wouldn't be now. Karen came bounding down the stairs to meet her and steer them outdoors immediately.

"Hi, Karen. Hold on. Could we sit down and get a drink of water?"

"No time! We'll get something on the way!" Karen said. "Is this the car?"

"Yep." She forgot what it was called. It was a car. And then she remembered a friend she'd had who'd had a car named Byron, for Lord Byron, her favorite poet. That made her smile. She got in to the car, and Karen got in on the other side. Kay had forgotten all about her thirst. She was eager for adventure.

Then she realized that she had no idea what the word "adventure" really meant. Something that occurs by chance? Fortune? Serendipity? Luck? That could mean anything. It could mean stepping out in front of a bus. So what? The word must mean more than that. A toast! To chance!

"You okay, Kay?" asked Karen.

"I sure am," said Kay. "I got a nice buzz going, and we are going to have fun! We are finally going to see the rest of this damned play!"

"Woohoo! Yes!" exclaimed Karen, getting into the spirit of things.

"Tell you what, though. Would you mind driving? I think I may be a little too into the spirit of things myself. Probably shouldn't drive."

"No. Leave the car here. This is a perfect parking space. How'd you even find it? You know how hard it is to finding parking around here? I'll call for a Lyft."

"Oh, that would be a great idea. We should go inside for a while while we while away the time waiting. We can have a glass of wine or something. You have some wine, right?"

Karen pointed to her phone. "No time. She said she'll be here in three minutes."

"Who?"

"The Lyft driver."

"That's amazing."

"They are amazing."

"That's why they need a better way of doing business with the company that has been hiring their labor."

"Okay, okay, okay. No politics tonight? Just fun, okay, Kay?"

A gold coast silver Genesis G90 pulled up, and they got in.

"Hi," said the driver politely.

Karen gave her an intersection with North Avenue that was vague enough that it wouldn't mean anything in particular. The Lyft driver had no reason to know what play they were going to see, anyway. She might be one of those judgmental, suburban Lyft drivers who would never stop to help an ailing Samaritan. Oh, wait, that wasn't how the parable went, anyway. Oh, never mind. The theatre was a stumbling distance from where they'd be dropped off.

The drive was driven in silent silence.

They stepped out of the Lyft at long last, and then they waited for the driver to leave before making their way half a block to the theatre.

They were, of course, back in their same loge seats. Kay had made certain of that right after she'd decided they needed to come back the third time in order to see the end of the play. Of course, the next available day for those seats was a few weeks after the previous time they'd gone, but they had *such* full lives to lead when they were not attending *plays* together, after all. Kay shook her head. She was getting too tangled up in thinking. The time had come to turn the mind off. Watching this play would be the perfect opportunity for that. What was going to happen with the Pissers' Theatre inside the Pissers' Theatre? Now *that* was a question. Or perhaps a conundrum. When something is turned in on itself, it's an ouroboros. Was there an inside to go into, or was it all just swirling down the toilet, which seemed to be some sort of central metaphor in the play. And not just a metaphor, but an environment. And as Kay's father had once said to her about something they were watching together on TV, "This story is taking me somewhere I would never want to go. Why would I want to see it?"

She'd wondered that herself, of course, because she was too self-critical. But hearing it from her father hurt. She'd been in-volved in the making of the show, not in a major way, of course, but in enough of a way that she was proud of having worked on it, and his dismissal stung. And he knew she'd worked hard on it. That was just how he was. He had little time for any sincere praise of her. He preferred to keep the praise to the acceptable surficial levels. But at least she heard herself called "princess" sans sincerity more than she heard herself called "mimosa," the cring-ing plant. Or the worst, *Clumzo*, which was his portmanteau of

96

"clumsy" and "Bozo," meant to hurt twice as much. What he'd been able to do to her was recruit her to his side in his criticism of her so that his criticisms became hers. She had a hard time overcoming that.

Inside, they hurried to the loge.

* * *

They passed Rayro, of course, but he hadn't seen them as far as they could tell. They hurried past where he was, with his back turned, talking to one of the concession workers. They found their seats and quickly settled in. The play was starting in about two minutes. Karen had argued for the skipping of the first act and most of the second because they'd already seen it, but Kay pointed out that the timing of the play was inconsistent because it depended on the bladders of the elderly. If the system were only the way it was in the inner play, then the play could be proceeding apace. Perhaps the play was right. The play within the play, that is. Time is unpredictable.

Now Kay wished she'd listened to some music by the Irène Schweizer Trio before going to the play. That usually bucked her up for anything. That a woman jazz musician in Germany in 1967 had vision as great as this still got to her. Listening to Irène helped her get through her divorce. Irène was largely self-taught, and so Kay would have to be.

She all of a sudden remembered that she in many ways thought the recording they did together live in Mannheim in 1990 was even better. Both Irène and Mani had grown so very much in the intervening years. But they were still amazing at hearing each other and playing to each other's strengths, which were substantial! Irène and Mani were ironic and manic in the Mannheim recording. It was a recording of two virtuosos absolutely loving their instruments so much that they are willing to improvise a conversation in tandem with another instrument that they considered an equal. This was a rare moment in music.

Oh, the next scene.

* * *

Scene III-5: The box office again

(HENRY and MARY are sitting at opposite sides of the desk.)

MARY

This is not working.

HENRY

Nope. We are going broke.

MARY

And we still haven't recovered my grandfather's book that was in the safe.

HENRY

Your grandfather's book? He published a book?

MARY

No, it was never published. But this was the hand-written manuscript of it. I was going to try to have it published.

HENRY

What kind of a book was it?

MARY

It was a kind of Victorian novel with ghosts and séances.

* * *

That was the moment that Rayro chose to appear on stage himself. He had been tired of being nothing but an usher, and he knew he had to do something big.

He bounded up the steps to the stage from the wings and careened center stage. He took the microphone, and in a very dramatic sort of way, swung the microphone around on its cord and caught it in his hand in a sort of pop singing star style, which was, of course, so out of character for him that he arrested the attention of the audience completely.

"I am sorry to have to announce this, everyone, but we have had a sudden change in the script and cast tonight, so please stay seated. You are in for a treat."

Karen and Kay looked at each other. What? What the heck did that mean?

There they sat, all ready to finally see the ending of the third act of the play they had tried to sit through three times, and now they would again be foiled in the attempt? What was happening? What dastardly plan was in store for them next?

Viewers, tune in again tomorrow to the same dastardly channel at the same dastardly crime time, and see the rest of the play!

No! That would not happen!

The play was all of a sudden something completely different. Different actors were on stage, and an entirely different tone was set. What had happened? Kay wondered if they'd been slipped some drug and had passed out, and when they'd reawakened here, back in their seats, they'd been there so long that the next night's performance was in progress. They had slept in their seats for an entire day, but no one had noticed them. Or they'd figured these two women were not important enough to bother with. Either way was offensive.

* * *

Mindy and Aloysius sat backstage and wondered what had happened to their cues. They'd left stage for the last break, both wanting to sit and have a drink or smoke or anything other than standing on stage and doing nothing.

What had happened? Had the play been usurped? They heard something that sounded completely different. This was not their play. How was this new play all of a sudden on stage instead of their own?

* * *

A guerilla theatre company had taken over the space to do their own guerilla play. Mary had heard of that. These guerilla theatre companies would just take over different spaces and do their own plays for a night, and then go somewhere else to do it. They called this "Pop-Up Theatre." They had enormous followings on social media, and people would wait until late in the day to get the news about where that night's performance would be. And then all those actors and fans would descend on the designated theatre and take it over for the night. But only for one night. They wanted to disrupt, but not destroy. And tonight was the Pissers' Theatre's turn. That was an honor, actually. It was like having a building painted on by Keith Haring. That would make it beautiful. But not everyone saw the beauty of guerilla theatre, especially Mary, whose money was invested pretty heavily into the play.

When she heard the play begin again without her, she knew it was not her play. How could it be? Should she call the police?

But then she began to recognize it. Certain turns of phrase seemed familiar. She had some faint recollection of some of the unusual cadence to the sentences. She remembered feeling delight before at certain euphonious collections of syllables.

No! It couldn't be! How could it be? But it was. It was, without a doubt, her grandfather's book, adapted and changed, to be sure, but it was his story, most certainly.

There it was. Taken from her and then regurgitated into her face. Disgusting. Snorts and wheezes, farts and cheeses. Wait, did the actor just mention "swampy meadows strewn with drowned shrew-mice and moles"? That was right from her grandfather's book!

Actually, dear, it wasn't. Mary heard the voice of her grandmother chiding her. She'd always hated when her grandmother chided her. *That's from J. Meade Falkner. Don't you recognize* Moonfleet?

No, but I'm getting seasick from the italics.

Your grandfather was a plagiarist, Mary, dear. He never published his book because he'd swiped it and couldn't face the truth.

What?

He'd been on the train when Falkner had gotten off, and he'd seen Falkner leave his book bag. One couldn't leave a bag unattended. That was unseemly. So picking it up and taking it home was the only logical option. Of course it had to be checked before being put in the trunk. It looked so boring that it had to be legit. He figured he'd have a way to monetize it somehow, but that never happened.

Grandma, is that you?

And then, just as suddenly, the feeling that her grandmother was nearby was gone, and Mary felt silly for having felt it. But then she heard this:

"I believe there never was boy yet who saw a hole in the ground, or a cave in a hill, or much more an underground passage, but longed incontinently to be into it."

That was definitely her grandpa. She heard his voice say those words as if they were coming to her from the backstage speakers.

Weren't they really his words? Was she hallucinating them? And how did he make his voice split into stereo, with one channel for his voice and the other for some background soundtrack music, something like the crisp, ambient music of Pauline Anna Strom?

"Do you hear those liquid ghost sounds coming from the music speakers?" Henry asked.

"I hear some ambient music," said Mary.

"That's not music. Listen closer. Turn the balance all the way to the music side of the mix. I think it's the left speaker control."

Mary went over to the sound console and turned the balance all the way to the left. Sure enough, the spoken lines of the play went silent, and all that could be heard was a strange, human-sounding gurgling. Maybe those were indeed liquid ghost sounds. She looked to see what was feeding into the stereo, and she traced the sounds to a Blu-ray device that someone had hooked up to the sound system. Both it and the stage mikes were being fed in simultaneously. She removed the disc and saw it was indeed labeled *Liquid Ghost Sounds*. Why would anyone have put that into the system?

A knock came on the office door. Henry opened the door, and Rayro walked in.

"What happened to the soundtrack? We need that for the play."

"Why?"

"It's a ghost story. That was J. Meade Falkner's specialty."

"What does J. Meade Falkner have to do with anything?"

"Oh, this is a play based on his fourth novel, the lost one."

"No, this is a play based on my grandfather's book, which was stolen from my safe."

"It wasn't stolen. It was liberated. And it wasn't your grandfather's book. It was by Falkner."

"I don't think so. It was in my grandfather's estate, and it is in his own handwriting."

"We examined that fact. The experts have concluded that the language is Falkner's, so your grandfather must have copied Falkner's manuscript himself. Perhaps your grandfather intended to return Falkner's manuscript, so he wanted to keep a copy for himself. Remember that photocopiers didn't exist back then."

"So where, then, is the original manuscript? And how do you know all this?"

Rayro looked slightly alarmed at the implications of the question. "I have a friend who studied Falkner in graduate school. She became quite familiar with his style, and then when a collector friend of ours took a look at it, he knew what we had."

"So you stole the manuscript?"

"No, not me. Not directly. And it wasn't stolen by us. It was stolen by your grandfather. We were just liberating it from its captivity. No one has the right to withhold great literature from the public."

"But why a play? Wouldn't a book have been more logical?"

"Oh, a book version is definitely in the works, but that's going to take some time. Meanwhile, since I have a theatre connection here and my friends have theatre connections elsewhere, we figured doing the play in pop-up performances would start to pique interest in the project."

"So you are behind the usurping of the stage tonight?"

"Yes, sort of, in cahoots with my friends."

"And who are these friends?"

"They call themselves the Poppy Weasel Theatre Company."

"Never heard of them."

"You will. They are a guerilla theatre company, and tonight is just the beginning of the pop-up plays they'll be doing."

"Oh, jeez Louise," said Henry. "Where are you taking this next?"

"I don't know. I am not involved in the next performance. I

was only involved in this one because of my connection to the theatre. But I suspect that the next one is going big, maybe one of the major downtown theatres."

"Good luck," said Henry. "They employ off-duty cops as security, and those cops don't mess around."

"Well, don't worry about that. All you have to worry about is tonight. After this, you will not see us here again."

"Well, you work here," said Mary.

"Not after tonight," replied Rayro.

"Well, you don't need to quit on my account," said Mary. "I like your ingenuity. Maybe we can figure out how to harness it within the theatre rather than against the theatre."

"I have nothing against the theatre at all. I really like working here."

"Okay, well, then, go finish your play." She reinserted *Liquid Ghost Sounds* in the Blu-ray player and rebalanced the channels.

Rayro nodded, turned, and exited.

After he was gone, Mary turned to Henry and said, "This may end up a blessing in disguise."

"Yes, at least you didn't have the book published to only be accused of fraud, like that Clifford Irving guy with his Howard Hughes book."

"That's true. But maybe we can find a way to have the notoriety that will come with tonight's usurpation invigorate our ticket sales."

"Hey, yes. Maybe we can even ask these Poopy Weasel people—"

"*Poppy* Weasel," corrected Mary.

"Whatever. Maybe they can do the show here regularly. That's got to be better than having to do pop-up theatre."

"Not sure. If they define themselves as 'guerilla,' then perhaps having a regular venue goes against their principles."

Henry nodded. "That could be."

* * *

Karen looked at Kay, who looked as mystified by the shift in the play as she was. Was all this an intentional part of the play? Was this a faux usurpation? Was this meant to be a commentary on the state of drama or of society as a whole?

They watched as the ghost story unwound, and this time they actually lasted until the denouement.

At the pub afterwards, over two glasses of Jameson's and two pints of Guinness, Kay and Karen debated what the play had been about. They were not entirely sure.

Kay argued that guerilla theatre was a real strategy, and what they had witnessed was an actual usurpation of an actual play by another actual play. It was a unique event, and so she and Karen should count their blessings to have been lucky enough to have been there. Kay explained how, when she had been younger and had lived in the city herself, she had gone to an artist's loft in the SuHu art district, and there a boxing ring had been set up. Two poets, Jerome Sala and Jim Desmond, fought a standard ten-round boxing match, each contestant having ninety seconds to present a poem. The winners were tallied round by round, and the crowd was as enthused as any for a Golden Gloves bout. The competition was keen, and Sala ended up supreme that night. That event, one of only three poetry boxing matches that were held in that loft before poetry competitions became poetry slams and moved to the Green Mill and elsewhere, was one that Kay had remembered ever since. This play, she claimed, would be just as permanently carved into their memories as the Sala/Desmond bout had been.

Karen didn't agree. She thought that this was all part of the play. She thought that the theft of the manuscript, the dubious claims for its authorship, and the performance of a play based on the lost manuscript were too contrived to be real. She argued that if this indeed were a true usurpation, why would the thieves return to the theatre whence they had absconded with the manuscript? No, she said, this was all some sort of meta-play, very postmodern. The bifurcation of the play into two halves, one about a Pissers' Theatre and the other about a stolen copy of a manuscript, attributed to J. Meade Falkner, whether correctly or not, and the subsequent performance of the play in the very theatre they had stolen the manuscript from, was simply too precious to be true.

Kay suggested that they wouldn't be able to know for sure unless they came back and watched the play again a fourth time.

Karen laughed loudly, but the bartender gave her a displeased scowl to let her know that such joviality had no place in his bar. So she stopped. "Sure," she said, "we should definitely do that!"

But neither woman really believed they would. They had ridden this play project of theirs to its logical conclusion, and now that the play was done, their excuse for getting together had come to an end. Months might pass before either would find or suggest another activity for them both together. So because this was the last time they'd see each other for a long while, they drank until closing time and then called for a ride to Karen's place. Kay was too drunk to drive, so she slept on Karen's couch. Kay was pretty much just in the door and collapsed, thanks to some careful steering by Karen. The couch was so uncomfortable that Kay had problems sleeping. At six o'clock she gave up. While Karen was still asleep, Kay fixed herself some strong coffee and toasted a croissant that she found in Karen's fridge. She saw a notepad on the fridge door, so she left a note for Kay: "Thanks for the great evening. I still think we should see the play again. Call me when you get a chance. Love you! Kay."

Kay quietly left the apartment, climbed into her car, which was not named Byron, and drove home.

ABOUT THE AUTHOR

Eckhard Gerdes has published books of poetry, drama, and fourteen novels, including *White Bungalows* and *My Landlady the Lobotomist*. He has won an &NOW Award, the Richard Pike Bissell Award, been a finalist for the Starcherone and the Blatt awards, and was nominated for Georgia Author of the Year. His most recent books include a tongue-in-cheek work of creative nonfiction, *How to Read*, and *Marco* and *Iarlaith: A Novel in Flash Fictions*. He is also editor and publisher of *The Journal of Experimental Fiction* and its associated imprint JEF Books. He lives near Chicago and has three children and five grandchildren.

2 + 2 = 5 Alphonse Allais
DOUBLE OVER Alphonse Allais
THE SQUADRON'S UMBRELLA Alphonse Allais
THE ALPHONSE ALLAIS READER
ALPHONSE ALLAIS'S MASKS Deluxe Special Edition
HIDDEN GEMS: THE BEST OF *THE PEARL* Anonymous
THE MAN WHO WALKED ON AIR Alain Arias-Misson
DANTE'S FOIL & OTHER SPORTING TALES Mark Axelrod
THE ZOMBIE OF GREAT PERU Pierre-Corneille de Blessebois
SWEET AND VICIOUS Suzanne Burns
SMELLS LIKE TEEN 'PATAPHYSICS Norman Conquest
COLLECTED MONOLOGUES Charles Cros
UPSIDE-DOWN STORIES Charles Cros
ANGEL OF EVERYTHING Catherine D'Avis
FROM THEIR LIPS TO HIS EARS Denis Diderot
TODAY IS THE DAY THAT WILL MATTER Debra Di Blasi
MARCO & IARLAITH Eckhard Gerdes
WEIRDLY OUT WEST Rhys Hughes
THE POPE'S MUSTARD-MAKER Alfred Jarry
THE RITES OF ECSTASY Hélène Lavelle
PATENTS PENDING Derek Pell & Doug Skinner
TRAVELS TO MERRYLAND Roger Pheuquewell, Esq.
THE SECRET OF GERANIUMS Jessy Reine
HERE LIES MEMORY: A PITTSBURGH NOVEL Doug Rice
THE PUPPET-PLAY OF DOCTOR GALL Jason E. Rolfe
THE UNKNOWN ADJECTIVE & OTHER STORIES Doug Skinner
SLEEPYTIME CEMETERY: 40 STORIES Doug Skinner
CRITICS & MY TALKING DOG Stefan Themerson
TOURIST: A NOVEL Temenuga Trifonova
THE NEW URGE READER 4 Various
LE SCAT NOIR ENCYCLOPÉDIE Various
LE SCAT NOIR BEDSIDE NONSENSE Various
THE BEST OF LE SCAT NOIR Various
OULIPO PORNOBONGO ANTHOLOGY Various
APRIL FIREBALL: EARLY STORIES Tom Whalen
CURIOUS IMPOSSIBILITIES Carla M. Wilson
THREE PLAYS BY D. HARLAN WILSON
VAHAZAR Witkacy